C000005678

3 month rota

at LUT	until...|||
at SHE	until... 3/8
at SYS	until... A
at ASH	until... /3//8
at BIR	until... 3//8
at BLA	until... |/8
at BRO	until...
at EAR	until... 0.1/20
at GLE	until...

2634 539

DAYS OF IGNORANCE

DAYS OF IGNORANCE

Laila Aljohani

Translated by Nancy Roberts

دار بلومزبري - مؤسسة قطر للنشر
BLOOMSBURY
QATAR FOUNDATION
PUBLISHING

مؤسسة قطر
Qatar Foundation

First published in English in 2014 by
Bloomsbury Qatar Foundation Publishing
Qatar Foundation
PO Box 5825
Doha
Qatar
www.bqfp.com.qa

First published in Arabic in 2007 as *Jahiliyya* by Dar Aladab, Beirut

Copyright © Laila Aljohani, 2007
Translation © Nancy Roberts, 2014

The moral right of the author has been asserted

ISBN 9789992195192

Typeset by Hewer Text UK Ltd, Edinburgh
Printed and bound by CPI Group (UK) Ltd, Croydon, CR0 4YY

Contents

I

A falling sky

According to senior officials in the US Administration, the White House is expected to announce today that Iraq has violated United Nations resolutions demanding that it disclose its weapons of mass destruction. The officials stated that President George Bush will discuss the matter in a special meeting of the National Security Council prior to the White House's announcement.

Munis * *the 15th of Wail,*
the twelfth year after Desert Storm
3 a.m.

Is he dead?

That night, in his agitation, he'd heard a sound that had shaken him to the core. When he looked at Malek's body, crumpled on the faded asphalt, alone, unarmed, assaulted without warning, he knew all the water on earth would never be able to wash away his transgression. He wept at the image that passed through his mind. He sobbed like a lost child. Sahar had wept several years earlier, but her tears hadn't troubled him at all. At the time he'd thought he wasn't moved because he was strong and hadn't done anything wrong. On the contrary – or so he'd thought – everything had been her choice, the way she'd wanted it. Now he realized it had nothing to do with strength. It was just cruelty. He'd been cruel, with the heart of a little demon that had kept leading him onward until it had brought him to this abyss.

Was Malek dead? How could he find out? Through Leen? When she'd looked over at him that night while his mother was wiping his head with water, crying and praying for God to protect him from accursed Satan, he'd been afraid she might understand. He found himself fleeing to his room. After all, how could he tell her, or ask her to tell him whether Malek was alive or dead?

3

If Malek had died, he would die, too. They'd be sure to punish him. When the news got out, people would spread all sorts of rumours. And when that happened, he'd have added another evil to the evil he had committed – a scandal!

O Lord! O Lord!

He began to cry. The object crouching on his chest grew heavier, and heavier, and heavier. A burning lump was choking him, and for a moment he felt he couldn't breathe. He didn't hear his mother come in. All he was aware of was the pain in his head, which he'd beaten against the wall. Then he saw his mother burying her face in her hands and crying before casting a look of searing reproach at the ceiling.

If he died, his mother would die too. She'd made him the pillar of her life, and the minute the pillar snapped, the sky would fall on her head. She didn't know yet what he'd done. But even if she found out, she'd understand why he'd done it, and she'd forgive him.

He looked at her as she sat across from him, paralyzed and helpless. He wished he could curl up in a ball and go back to being an unborn child inside her womb. Why had he even been born? If only she'd miscarried him like the others before him! He smelled the aroma of her body mingled with the fragrance of her perfume. She smelled like a mother. He didn't know how the thought had occurred to him, but it did occur to him, and it crushed him: maybe Malek hadn't died, and maybe he had a mother who was crying over him. But now he would be unconscious, unable even to perceive that his mother was weeping over his head.

4

2

And he never saw any angels

The Pentagon has stated that it has no information regarding the alleged transfer of US troops and equipment from Turkey to northern Iraq despite reports to this effect by Turkish news channel NTV and Al Jazeera satellite channel. A Pentagon spokesman in Washington said, 'I have nothing on this.' A Turkish military spokesman declined to comment on statements made by NTV. A US Embassy official in Ankara told Reuters, 'I haven't heard anything. There is no evidence in support of the NTV report.' Al Jazeera quoted Turkish military sources as saying that fifty US military trucks had begun transferring equipment on Saturday from an air base in southern Turkey into three Kurdish-controlled regions in northern Iraq. According to the Al Jazeera report, the trucks used the Khabur border gate.

Jubar ★ *the 13th of Wail,*
the twelfth year after Desert Storm
4 a.m.

He wished he would die. However, he didn't realize he wished it. Everything around him seemed vague and uncertain. He didn't know anymore whether he was dead or alive. He heard the sound of metal grating against metal without being able to stop his ears. The sound disturbed him. But what disturbed him even more was the fact that he couldn't understand what had happened to him.

Many faces passed through his darkness, but he could only make out a few of them. One of them was Leen's face, which looked captivating to him at that moment. He wished he could reach out and touch her cheek. The last time he'd tried to touch it, she'd shied away from him like a frightened gazelle. He remembered that she'd been distressed. But he didn't remember whether she'd gotten over her distress or not. She smiled warmly, in her eye a glint he didn't know how to interpret. The blood flowed thick and warm out of his nose, and its saltiness settled along the sides of his tongue. He remembered her licking his shoulder once and saying, 'You taste salty.' He wanted to smile, but he didn't know whether he could smile again or not. Tiny colored lights glistened in his darkness, while stars with phosphorescent hues – red, green, and yellow – and spiral-shaped creatures descended from the top of the darkness to the bottom, gliding like luminous sea creatures in the depths of a lightless ocean. He heard frantic footsteps, shouts, curses and insults. But something kept him from understanding what had happened to him.

He thought about the fact that his ribs were hurting. Suddenly they'd become like blazing splinters implanted in the flesh of his chest. He heard his feeble heartbeats. Then he saw his mother waving to him in the distance. He wished he could run toward her and ask, 'What's wrong with me, Mother? Touch me so that I can know what's wrong with me!'

But he didn't run. He kept trying to call her without knowing if he'd really called her or not. There was no sky above him, there was no earth beneath him, nor was he floating on water. He was in limbo between this world and the next, but he didn't see any angels.

He was trying not to die, but he didn't know whether he was succeeding or not. Of all the things that had broken his spirit, the one that had hurt the most was loneliness. When he'd closed his eyes for the last time, his loneliness had destroyed him. It terrified him to realize with such certainty that his loneliness was all he had left. Even Leen had been transformed in a moment into an illusion, and he couldn't understand how things had reached this point. He'd been beaten mercilessly, and pain had left his spirit in tatters. Pain, humiliation, and the bitter sense of having been duped. What had happened to him? Why had it happened? And who had done it?

A voice had shouted, 'That's enough!', and at that moment his consciousness had begun seeping away.

At that point he'd stopped seeing anything but darkness. He'd stopped feeling anything but cold and a horrible loneliness. He waited a long time for the angels to come. But they never did.

3

Silence and death

The United States has sent dozens of teams composed of special forces and intelligence specialists into Iraq. It has supplied them with millions of dollars in liquid funds to entice tribal leaders to distance themselves from President Saddam Hussein. The British newspaper the *Observer* mentioned in a report yesterday that this covert campaign – which relies on methods used successfully in Afghanistan last year – began several weeks ago, and is an important part of the military and political strategy being pursued by the United States and its close ally, Britain, to strip Saddam of his weapons of mass destruction or to change the ruling regime in Baghdad.

Ahwan * the 12th of Wail, the twelfth year after Desert Storm

King Faysal Street

God damn the animal. He's worse than an animal. And God damn her. She's an animal, too.

He would always say she was an animal. If only his mother had suffocated her after she was born. If only she'd died instead of the others that had died before him. If only God had said, 'Kill her.' But killing her would bring her relief, and he didn't want her to have any relief. He wanted her to suffer for a good long time. The animal! If only her father had given him authority over her. If only he hadn't come between them. If only . . . if only . . . if only . . .

If only what? Like, what would I have done then?

She was stronger than him. He had to admit that, at least. Whenever he glared at her, all she did was smile serenely, then go back to what she'd been doing. That serenity of hers killed him! Even when he shouted in her face, all she did was let him go on shouting, without thinking of shouting back. And when she found him searching her room, what had she done? Had she lost her temper? Had she shouted in his face? No, no, no. All she'd done was stand there, leaning on the doorframe with her arms folded over her chest. She'd stood there watching him as he left her room, flustered, without having found a shred of evidence to justify to his father the way he'd been raging against her. He hadn't taken any photo

11

or letter that he could fling in his father's face, saying, 'Look what I found in her room, Dad! See it with your own eyes, and don't make excuses for her. Your daughter's going to cause us a scandal!' He hadn't taken anything, and as he left the room, he had tried to avoid looking her in the eye. He was sure that if he went back to her room today, he'd find that she'd put her things back in their usual places, and that she wouldn't think of trying to hide them. If only he knew where she got that strength. It was as if it didn't matter to her whether anybody – even his father – found out what was going on between her and the animal. Did his father know what was going on between them?

Damn!

She'd even had the audacity to inform his father! And why not? He loved her. He really did love her. He loved her in a way that he, her brother, couldn't understand. He couldn't stand it, and he suspected that his father 'understood' the situation. 'Understanding' – that beloved word of his!

'Try to understand your sister's situation, Hashem, and accept her the way she is. I know my daughter, so you should try to know your sister. Don't be her enemy just because you're a man and she's a woman. Why do you think your being a man means you have to harass her?'

His sister, his sister, his sister! Did he have to have a sister? A woman who was neither his mother nor his lover? A woman he could neither trust nor amuse himself with? A woman his father refused to give him the authority over to keep her from doing herself harm? His father was depriving him of the authority to protect her from what he knew of the world around him. Here was a woman whose mistakes he was supposed to understand and tolerate no matter what. He was supposed to watch

12

her fall, then encourage her to get up again. What kind of a man was his father, anyway? How could he stand knowing that his only daughter was in a relationship with a man? And what man? What man? He'd never be able to hold his head up again. He'd never be able to do that unless he did something to stop them.

God damn her, and God damn him. God damn her whole kind. And the animal, I suppose he can't believe his good luck.

Sitteen Street

Why wasn't time passing?!

Bleep, bleep, bleep.

The speeding alarm was going off. He looked at the alarm light out of the corner of his eye, thinking: Why can't ordinary cars go 500 km/hr?

That would be great. Nobody would have to suffer. People would die just like that. Imagine just one car going 500 km/hr and crashing into another one. B-o-o-o-o-o-m! Certain death. But never mind. Even 200 km/hr isn't bad!

Y-e-a-h . . .

If only he could climb the age ladder at that speed so that the age difference between them would be on his side, so that, if even just once, he could be the eldest. If only . . . But 'if only' wasn't going to do any good now. His mother had made a mistake by having her so many years before she'd had him. That's right, she'd made a mistake. When he told her this, she'd laughed and said, 'I saved the best till last!'

She was older than he was, but it wasn't often that she'd shouted in his face, and never once had she scolded him. Not even when she'd found him hunting pigeons on the roof of their house. She'd gotten a sad look on her face that day when

13

she saw a slingshot in his hand and a wounded pigeon nearby. She'd said, 'Medina is a sanctuary, Hashem. Hunting its pigeons isn't allowed.'

'You think I'm the only one in the whole city who hunts them? All the kids hunt them and raise them.'

'All right, then. Buy yourself a couple of pairs from the pigeon market. Then you won't need to hunt them.'

'Why should I buy them when the sky is full of them?'

Before leaving, she looked at him with a perplexed half-smile on her face and said, 'It's wrong for you to hunt them, Hashem, when we live so close to the holy precincts.'

Then she went downstairs. That had happened a long time ago. He'd been a young boy at the time. She would speak to him every now and then, the way she did about the pigeons, then go her way. He'd realized early on that she was unimpressed with a lot of the things he did. She would often complain about his behavior to their mother. But their mother would just shut her up, saying, 'Let him do whatever he wants.'

So she'd grudgingly let him be. Now, too, he was going to do whatever he wanted, and he wasn't going to let *her* be. Nor would his mother say, 'Let her do whatever she wants.' No. She'd never said it in the past, and she wasn't going to say it now. Instead she'd say, 'Do whatever you want. Defend your honor!'

She'd say a lot of things. But he needed to finish the job first, then go back to her. He wouldn't talk to her about the pigeons. He'd search Leen's room again, and he'd take what he hadn't taken the first time. His father wasn't going to stand between them this time, and if he tried to, he wasn't going to keep his mouth shut. His father didn't realize what kind of a predicament his 'understanding' might land them in. He hadn't experienced what his son had, and he didn't know what his son did. His good-hearted father had lived his youth without going through anything to speak of. What did his father know about women and their minds? How was he supposed to know he couldn't trust a woman no matter how mature she happened to be? After all, a single word might numb her mind and wipe it out as though it had never existed.

Airport Road

He smiled to himself. His father could never imagine how many women he'd known. He'd been busy with them for years. God damn them. What would life be like if God hadn't made them? How had his life gotten so confused now because He'd made them? If only He'd created them without their having anything to do with anybody. If only He'd made it so that they weren't mothers, sisters or wives. If only He'd made them for nothing but enjoyment!

W-o-o-o-o-o-w.

If that were the case, he would only use his car for the sake of being with a woman. The two of them would have a good time for a while, then go their separate ways without a care. He'd never have to worry about his sister, wondering where she'd gone, who she'd gone to see, who she'd gone with, when she'd gone, or how she'd gone.

Ugh . . .

His sister! His sister, who wanted the . . . to lay her . . .

The animal. Do you suppose he's done it? No . . .!!

C – r – a – s – h!

'God damn you. Where did *you* come from?'

Be careful, Hashem. Be careful! You nearly died just now because you were thinking about that animal. But he's the one who ought to die, not you!

He slowed down and pulled over to the side of the road. He picked up a bottle and began wiping his face with water from it before taking a drink. He took a deep breath. He looked around for a while, pondering the stores along the right side of Airport Road. As he pulled out onto the road again, he could see he needed to leave these thoughts aside. If he went on thinking this way, he'd never do anything. He'd never do what he had in mind.

He needed to think about other things that didn't make him so tense. He turned in to the Falah Station and pulled up in front of the gas pump. He asked the attendant to fill up the tank. Neither of them smiled. Nobody smiled at anybody. Everybody looked glum. He saw his furrowed brow in the rear-view mirror, but it didn't occur to him to soften his facial expression. The sun's glaring rays reflected harshly off the metal of the cars passing by. The air around him was heavy with the smell of gasoline.

He gazed at his car's leather interior. He remembered the first time he'd touched it. When had that been? At least two years earlier. That's right. He'd been happy as he inspected it. As he ran his hands over one part after another, a vague sense of exhilaration had come over him. Before that he'd had a used Caprice. He hadn't been happy with it. But he hadn't been miserable with it either. He just wished he had a big fancy car like lots of other guys he knew. For a long time he'd dreamed of having a Porsche. But that would be a luxury he couldn't come by easily. At other times he'd dreamed of having a yellow Ferrari that would catch people's eye. But we don't always get the things we dream of. He cursed high school, which hadn't been what he'd hoped for, and his silly diploma. Even more, he cursed Fortune for not making his father rich. And now he was leaving the gas station cursing his sister and the moment he'd become a brother.

He's laid her. The animal's laid her! He's laid her.

And he? How had he failed to notice? He'd been busy laying other women.

'What goes around comes around, Hashem. You've got a sister, and some day you'll be sorry.'

That was what Sahar had said one evening before getting out of his car for the last time some years earlier. He'd heard a tearful tremor in her voice, but he hadn't done anything. Everything she'd done, she'd done of her own free will. He hadn't forced her to do anything. He hadn't promised her anything. He'd thought he was in love with her, but as soon as the blood flowed between her thighs, everything was over. The thrill of getting to know her was gone. The longing to touch her was gone. Even the pleasure of looking at her pretty face was gone. What he'd been looking for or expecting wasn't there anymore. He kept thinking to himself: *She's easy, easy. She opened her door too quickly.* He hadn't been able to tell her that he'd been ridden with misgivings, just the way he'd ridden her, because she hadn't resisted long enough, because she'd opened the door to her house, saying, 'Come on in. Nobody's home.'

When, the first time, he'd tried to kiss her, she hadn't gotten angry. When, the second time, he'd reached out to touch her, she'd smiled. And by their third meeting, she was moaning under him with a strange expression on her face that almost made her ugly. But he hadn't been concerned about that, since it hadn't been important for her to be pretty at that moment.

His relationship with her hadn't lasted long. Just a few weeks. Then it had all been over. He'd met her for the last time in response to her insistent pleading. She looked as though she'd just recovered from some protracted illness. Her eyes were sunken, her face was ashen, and she wasn't pretty anymore. But he hadn't wanted to think about what or who had changed. For a long time she didn't say a word. But it didn't occur to him to break her silence with a passing question about her, or about anything else for that matter. He tightened his grip on the steering wheel, waiting for her to say something, anything. But she didn't say a word. She just cried. Then she blurted out those words of hers: 'What goes around comes around,' and hurriedly got out of the car. He never heard about her again. He never saw her. He didn't even try to ask about her. And why would he have tried? She wasn't the way she'd been before. She wasn't the rowdy girl he'd met one evening on Quba' al-Nazil Street after just two telephone conversations.

She'd said, 'I'll wait for you on the sidewalk on the right side of the street, across from the Ahli Bank. I'll be carrying a small white purse.'

When she settled onto the seat next to him, he'd begun to tremble. It was his first time. He'd been afraid she would notice how flustered he was. He squeezed the steering wheel as hard as he could. In the meantime, he took another look at the white purse without saying a word, waiting for her to say something.

'If you aren't going to say hello for my sake, say it for God's sake at least, you . . .!'

He breathed a sigh of relief. The purse was white, and this was her voice. *Her* voice. That's right, hers. Even so, his stomach started doing flip flops. By this time they'd left Quba' al-Nazil Street and were headed up the Safiya Bridge, and he was afraid his insides would give out on him.

God damn streets that don't have any public bathrooms!

When the car headed down the bridge in the direction of al-'Awali, he pulled over, making some excuse he couldn't remember anymore. Then he ran off in search of somewhere he could do what he needed to do. No sooner had he returned than half his fears had been allayed. She was still waiting for him. She didn't say anything, and neither did he. She was still breathing calmly and deeply. He thought to himself: Maybe she's from the secret police. But he resisted the silly idea. Maybe she'd noticed how flustered he was. Then she uncovered her face, turned to him calmly and said, 'Damn you. So all you think of when you're with me is going to the bathroom?'

He laughed. That was just what he'd needed to calm him down: laughter. He pulled over again, still laughing. Then he said, 'Would you believe I thought you were with the secret police?'

She started with fright. 'My God, what a horrible thing to think! Lord, keep them in their places! What on earth gave you an idea like that?'

He laughed again. Then they took off. He drove her all over the city that day. He sped like crazy with her sitting beside him, talking her head off and laughing as though she'd known him for years. He took her to Sultana Street, where they drove up and down. She told him how much she hated the traffic light in front of Amer's Furniture Store.

'You nearly have a heart attack waiting for it to turn green,' she quipped.

Then they took off for Al Jamiat Road, where they drove slowly along the wall of the King Abdulaziz University. Its paint was peeling off, and its color had faded from having the sun beat down on it for so long. She told him her dream was to finish high school as fast as she could so that she could go to the university. There was a sweet tone in her voice. He looked at her thoughtfully, and was startled to see how pretty she looked when she spoke with such joyful abandon. Her eyebrows were fine and arched. Her eyes were small, but they were captivating when she turned suddenly or looked down, showing her thick eyelashes. She didn't have a beautiful nose, but it seemed to fit her face. As for her lips, they were tantalizingly full. Above them there was a slight moustache, and he remembered being bothered that day by her lack of concern to get rid of it. As he sat there looking at her, he didn't know how he felt about her.

Had he loved her? Love wasn't something he'd been looking for at the time. And he wasn't looking for it now, either. He'd often wondered whether he would ever love a woman. Besides, what was love? Why was it that when he asked this question, he found no answer? And why did it bother him – sometimes, at least – not to find an answer? Of all the women who'd passed through his life, which of them had he loved, if even just a bit? All the women he'd known – the tall ones and the short ones, the thin ones and the fat ones, the shy ones and the forward ones, the ones looking for love and the ones just looking for a good time – all of them had come and gone without pain, regret, or . . . hope. He'd forgotten a lot of them. They'd fallen through the cracks in his memory.

So why hadn't he forgotten Sahar? Maybe it was because a man doesn't forget his first time, or his first woman. He hadn't forgotten her. But afterwards he'd decided to be careful, and only to go after the ones who were just looking for a good time, especially married women, since none of them demanded any love and devotion. With them he could be sure there wouldn't be any headaches. They knew what they wanted, and what he wanted. So as soon as boredom set in, the party would break up and it would be, 'So long, have a nice life.'

Al Hizam Street

Ayman didn't tell him what they'd do with the animal once they'd hunted him down. He said to him, 'First we get hold of him. Then we'll see what we're going to do.'

He couldn't tell him everything. He told him the animal was a relative of one of the girls at the care home where his sister worked, and that he'd harassed her on the job. That was all he had needed to say to make Ayman's blood boil.

'Don't worry,' Ayman said. 'We'll teach him a lesson.'

Ayman volunteered to make enquiries about the animal so that they could find out the details of his daily life. Once Hashem had shown him where he lived, it wasn't difficult to ask about him and keep an eye on him. There was nothing exciting about his daily routine – no late nights out, and no friends to speak of apart from two or three who came to see him from time to time.

And she was like him. The details of her life were few. Sometimes he wondered what she liked besides books. Was reading the only thing she enjoyed? She hardly took interest in making herself up, so how could she possibly lure a man? What had attracted him to her? And what would they talk about – she and the animal – if all she did was read? He compared her often to the women he'd known, and wondered if there was any man who would pay any attention to her. Based on what he knew about women and the women he'd known, she wasn't a woman. His sister wasn't like a single one of them. She'd tried to get closer to him, but her attempts had failed, perhaps because he and she were like parallel lines that can never meet. He couldn't understand how she looked at life. He found no enjoyment in the books she would hand him with a smile, saying, 'Try to read one of them, at least. I picked out one I thought you'd like.'

But nothing she chose ever pleased him. He'd read a few lines out of two or three of them, then set them aside. He had no time or patience for cold, lifeless words. His time belonged to him, not to books. His time belonged to the things he liked to do, not to pages filled with words whose authors would die before anybody had taken any notice of them. And she would die, too – not now, but later.

She'll die a slow death. Heh, heh, heh. Sweet idea: a slow death. Sweet and bitter. The remnants of schoolwork.

Y-e-a-h.

How many years had it been since he'd stopped going to school? Three years. God! Three years had passed since he'd graduated by sheer luck, but he hadn't found a college that would admit him. It had seemed bad at first, but it didn't seem that way anymore. He'd gotten used to it. Everything's livable once you get used to it. Besides, what would he have done with a degree? Put it in a plastic cover and stick it in a drawer in his room like thousands of others who'd graduated years ago and who were still unemployed?

22

When Hashem had been unemployed for nearly two years, his mother had pressed his father to find him a job – any job – to occupy his time until something came along for him. So his father rented one of the numerous little kiosks located along the northern wall of Al Baqi' Cemetery and filled it with souvenirs, prayer beads and prayer rugs. When his father told him about the kiosk, he was gripped with melancholy. He felt as though he'd been buried under a mountain of ice. He couldn't say no. At the same time, he went on thinking all night about what he would do in a kiosk selling souvenirs to pilgrims along a cemetery wall. By the end of the week the depression had made him ill. One night he came home late and headed to where his mother sat waiting for him. He buried his face in her lap and said, 'I'm not going back to the kiosk. I'm going to die.'

The next day his father stood at the door to his room. Without a trace of reproach in his voice, he said, 'Regret doesn't do any good, son. Your mother didn't do you a favor by being so solicitous toward you. And I didn't do you a favor by letting her raise you however she pleased. But I want to give you another chance so that I won't feel I've wronged you.'

He didn't specify what kind of chance it was he wanted to give him. But two weeks later he found out. One evening his father took him to a large store that sold perfumes and women's accessories in one of Medina's markets. After explaining to him that he'd be working as a salesman, he left him there. It wasn't bad at all. By the time the first half hour had passed, he knew he wouldn't be bored. How could he be bored in a place that was full of women? In the kiosk also he would have been encountering women of all sorts. Once, when he'd complained to a friend of how miserable he was in the kiosk, the friend had told him, 'Listen, boy. To get a peek at all those women is the chance of a lifetime. And you're telling me you're depressed?! God had you in a little paradise! You should have waited till the pilgrimage season. That's when things really get good. You would have been making your living off all sorts of women: Algerians, Moroccans, Syrians . . .'

But he hadn't been able to bear it. He and death didn't get along. How could he stand to have death right on the other side of the wall? How could he stand to see funeral processions coming from the Jibril Gate toward Al Baqi', or to hear people praying over the dead two or three times a day? In the accessory shop, by contrast, death never passed by. Eyes passed by. Lips passed by. Hands passed by. Bodies passed by. But death didn't pass by.

What had brought death along? Let it stay away. That's right. Let death go on lurking on one of Medina's back streets waiting for the animal. But did he want the animal to die? Did he really want him to die? He didn't know. When he thought about it, something burned inside him, and he was sure that the minute he saw him, he would murder him. That's right. Death was the gentlest of all the ideas that came to his mind. He thought of digging his teeth into his flesh, scratching up his face, dragging him through the streets. He'd ruminated on it for nights on end. And every time he thought about it, the scene in his mind got more brutal, but his rage didn't subside. He didn't want to hurt him just once, but over and over. He wished he could have a chance to torture him at length. That's right. He wanted to torture him for as long as he'd been consumed by this thing that blazed deep inside him but that he couldn't name. If he had a chance, he'd cauterize him with a hot branding iron. He'd pour boiling water on him. He'd kick him between the thighs. That's right. He'd kick him over and over again till the animal knew where his limits were. He heaved a slow sigh. At least he knew he'd kick what was between his thighs. He had a chance to do it, and nobody was going to stop him. Who would stop him? Lots of people would think the same way if they knew what he knew. If they knew about it, all his friends would support him. They'd pounce with him on the animal and beat him to death.

Quba' al-Nazil Street

He noticed that silence had been dogging him ever since he'd turned off the radio so that the attendant at the gas station on Airport Road could fill his tank. Silence dogged him as he left the station. It dogged him as he drove down the city streets: King Faysal Street, Airport Road, Hizam Street, King Abdulaziz Street. And now he was heading down Quba' al-Nazil Street in silence, which was one of many things he didn't like in this life. He didn't like silence. He didn't like silence to be alone with him, just as he'd never liked death to be nearby, and never would. When he went to sleep he didn't turn off the TV in his room. Instead he would turn it down, leaving it on just high enough to make him feel that somebody else was around and that the universe wasn't yet empty. Then he'd go to sleep. In the beginning his mother had come into his room late at night to turn the TV off so that it wouldn't bother him. However, she stopped when she saw his reaction, which indicated that he actually wanted it on. She realized that this was another of her son's peculiar habits, and that she would have to reconcile herself to it the way

25

she'd reconciled herself to his other habits – like eating rice with bread, only taking a bath in the morning, not wanting anyone to talk to him after he woke up until all his senses were functioning one hundred percent, and not wanting to be touched by anybody he didn't know. She'd been worn out by this last idiosyncrasy of his when he was a little boy, and he had embarrassed her on many an occasion when other people were around. If anybody kissed him, he would grab his clothes, or his mother's clothes, and irritably wipe off the place where the kiss had been planted.

It might have felt strange to be surrounded so entirely by silence, but the loudness of the thoughts that filled his head had kept him from noticing it. Now, though, he did notice it. He noticed a silence that was interrupted by nothing but the roar of his car engine and the other cars passing by. He extended his index finger and turned on the radio, and the car was filled with the upbeat music that always came on before the MBC FM news broadcast. News?!

What was on the news other than slaughter and portents of war? For the first time he noticed that he was tense, and that what felt like a heavy stone lay on his chest. He wished everything could be over quickly. But the things a person doesn't like are never over quickly. If he'd been spending this time with one of his lady friends, it would have passed like a dream. But he wasn't dreaming. He was awake, furious, and silent, listening to the news:

. . . According to interested parties, the Iraqi opposition conference being held in London for the past two days, which has thus far been unable to overcome differences between the various factions, has decided to extend its

meetings today specifically in order to discuss the formation of committees that will be assigned the task of
managing the country after the potential fall of Iraqi
President Saddam Hussein's regime.

Mohamed ElBaradei, Director-General of the
International Atomic Energy Agency, has stated that UN
experts are making progress in Iraq, and has called on
Baghdad to continue cooperating in order to avoid the
outbreak of war.

A Japanese warship fitted out with an advanced Aegis
missile-detection system is headed for the Indian Ocean
today in a controversial move which, according to some
analysts, points to support for any potential US-led attack
on Iraq.

He thought of turning the radio off, but then thought better
of it. Before long the news broadcast would be over and songs
would come on. He wanted to hear some singing so that he
could calm down, if even just a little, before finishing the job,
then go home. If he had to wait, he would wait. However, he
knew that once it was done, he would go home. He wasn't
going to spend the night out. No. He wasn't going to wash
his hands anywhere but in his own house. He was going to act
according to the dictates of the situation. Then he would
think about what he was going to do with *her*. After all, she
was his sister, and he wasn't going to beat her. Even if he
thought of doing that, his father wouldn't allow it, and he
might beat him in punishment for it. He wouldn't beat her.
But he knew how to give her a taste of something more painful than a beating. First he had to finish *him* off, and then he
would have time to deal with her.

God damn her! Wasn't she bothered by his smell? Everybody of his race gave off a pungent, obnoxious odor. Hadn't she noticed it? You could smell one of them a mile away. How could she not have noticed?

He remembered a boy named Musa who'd been his classmate in eighth grade. He remembered how he'd avoided him the entire school year. He'd avoided all contact with him, even looking him in the eye. Musa's eyes were always red, and that was what had frightened him. Fags' eyes are red. For a long time he'd seen Musa hovering around certain boys, and it terrified him, since he himself was no fag.

Besides, he had that pungent, obnoxious smell like everybody else of his race. It was most noticeable when he sweated, as though his body gave it off especially at those times. But Musa had gone away, and after that school year he'd never seen him again. Two years later he'd heard that he was in prison. He hadn't been surprised. A lot of them seemed to end up there. The ones that weren't good at playing ball or singing were good at committing crimes.

Maybe the animal had escaped playing ball, singing and living a life of crime and was good at something else. But that didn't make him any different from the rest of them. And it would never mean that he had the right to breach his limits and aspire to things he wasn't entitled to. Wasn't he satisfied with what he'd achieved so far?

God damn him, and God damn her! After all, she was the one who'd started the whole thing. But everything would go back to normal. Everything. At least that was what he could think about now. How? He didn't know. However, he'd be sure to make things go back to the way they had been in the beginning, and to do what he hadn't had a chance to do before. If he couldn't, he'd invent a new beginning to his relationship with his sister. This way, things wouldn't get out of his control, and he wouldn't find himself in another mess he didn't know how to get out of.

Quba' al-Tali' Street

Would it be possible for me to make a new start?

The question shot through his mind like a bullet. He breathed deeply, and his nostrils were filled with a mysterious fragrance. He'd often wondered, almost hopelessly, whether he had anything to look forward to. He wasn't bitter about his life. In the end, though, it wasn't a life he could depend on: without a degree, without a job. He often claimed it didn't matter to him. But deep down, it did matter to him. When he compared his life to his sister's, he felt himself being stabbed by something small and hot. Her life was certainly not to his liking. But it had meaning – or so it seemed to him – since she had something to do, something to look forward to, something to dream of. It didn't seem to him that she enjoyed her life away from her books and her work. However, she didn't seem dissatisfied. Sometimes he suspected that she was never bored. When he saw her engrossed in her papers or books, writing or reading, or sitting at her computer screen reviewing something she'd written, he envied her, since he realized that she did what she did out of pure enjoyment. There was nothing in his life that he enjoyed that much. He didn't even enjoy girls that much. Once he'd emptied his semen into one of them, he would withdraw without even a thought of coming back to her again. It was like a burden he was happy to be rid of, and beyond that, nothing mattered to him anymore. For a long time he'd thought he must be abnormal to feel this way – not to enjoy what he went running after with such gusto. But when he asked some of his friends about it, he discovered that they were just like him. Unlike him, however, they weren't worrying about it. 'You get the hots for her, you try her out, and that's that!' That's what they told him. And that's what he kept trying to convince himself of. But deep down, he knew it wasn't really that way, and that it shouldn't be that way. He knew that if there was something wrong, the fault lay not in things, but in the way he did things.

One evening his sister had said to him, 'Show some fear of God in the way you treat people's daughters, Hashem.'

But if God had given him this body and planted in it this burning desire, how could he help giving in to it? Should he get married? No! He had too much sense to tie himself down to a single woman at his age. Besides, how was he supposed to get married when he had no job and no hope of finding one? He hadn't gotten married since there were women willing to give him their bodies at reasonable prices, and sometimes they settled for nearly nothing. There were women you could pick up on Sultana Street, Quba' Street, or King Faysal Street. One of them would get in the car and, if she didn't like the price – though most of the time she would agree to it – she would either get out or bargain a little.

He remembered the little girl he'd picked up one evening on Sultana Street. He'd been happy that nobody in his family was at home. He'd driven her back to the empty house and taken her to his room, but when she uncovered her face, he was shocked to discover how young she was. He guessed she wasn't more than fifteen years old. She'd plastered her eyes with kohl and painted her cheeks and

30

lips. Even then, she looked to him like some little girl who'd snuck into her mother's room when she wasn't looking and spattered her face with cosmetics. A wave of warm affection for her came over him. Seating her in front of him, he took a packet of tissues and began wiping her face. When she objected, he told her he didn't like make-up. How he'd lied! He'd wanted desperately not to touch her. However, she stripped and flung herself down on the bed, waiting for him. (*If she's only fifteen years old now, since when has she been working as a prostitute?*) The question kept going through his mind, but he didn't dare ask it, maybe because he didn't want to hear what he already knew, or what he'd guessed. He hurriedly satisfied himself with her, then got up quickly and put his clothes on. Wanting to get her out of the house before his parents or sister came home, he waited impatiently as she got dressed and ready to leave. But no sooner had they started down the hallway between his room and the small inner parlor than he saw his sister coming in their direction. She let out a short gasp when she saw them, the expression on her face a mixture of bewilderment and shock. It seemed she was so upset that she didn't know what to do or say. She quickly looked the other way and went to her room. Late that night, she opened the door to his room and said in an offended tone of voice, 'Fear God in the way you treat people's daughters, Hashem. Leave your dirty messes outside the house, not for my sake, but for Mom and Dad's sake.'

Then she shut the door behind her. He hadn't needed her to say that. He already knew he would never do it again. Never again would he bring somebody to the house only to discover in the end that she was a child – a mere child.

He drove down Qurban Street, and everything was ready for him. For hours he'd been gripping the steering wheel, driving around aimlessly just to pass the time, and now he felt a little tired. He slowed down and pulled over near some cars whose owners had turned them into vegetable and fruit stands. He turned off the engine and opened the car door, and the air came rushing inside. When he stood up his bones cracked, and the wind caused his robe to billow. He stretched a bit, thinking about a glass of tea. It pleased him to see that he felt like indulging in his everyday routines in spite of everything. He walked around his car and inspected it. Then he got in again and sat there watching the world around him.

As soon as it was time, he'd call Ayman, and they'd decide what to do. He had a lot of confidence in Ayman, his old neighbor and schoolmate. They'd parted ways during high school, but hadn't lost touch. They'd continued to get together from time to time, and had spent quite a number of days together. They'd also pulled stupid pranks that they were sure to laugh about later on.

He'd hesitated when it first occurred to him to ask for Ayman's help. He didn't know what he'd say to him, or how he would say it. However, his hesitation was short-lived. He'd been rehearsing the story, and as soon as Ayman heard part of it, he expressed his willingness to lend a hand. Consequently, there'd been no need to relate the details he'd invented, which had come as a big relief to him. In fact, it had relieved him of having to say much of anything at all. He'd been afraid there might be gaps in his story, that Ayman might ask questions, or that he might notice how flustered he was, how jumbled his words were, or how unsteadily he spoke.

However, Ayman's unbridled impulsiveness made things simpler for him. He didn't ask about any details, and he took no notice of Hashem's uneasiness. Instead, as soon as he began telling him the story he'd made up about the way the animal had harassed his sister, Ayman was gripped by a rage that reminded Hashem of the rage that had gripped him when he discovered what he'd discovered. All that remained was for the two of them to carry out what they'd set their minds to. They hadn't decided on anything in particular or laid out any plan, but their thoughts always moved in the same direction, and they still had enough time to exchange opinions.

He hadn't eaten lunch, but he wasn't hungry. All he wanted was some hot tea, preferably with mint, possibly on account of all the thoughts that had been raging in his head for the last few hours, as well as the thoughts, if there were any, that would be raging in his head in the hours to come.

Ayman was waiting for him. As for Hashem, he was waiting to get his hands on the animal. He ground his teeth. He was still seething, and the heavy stone was still weighing on his chest. But he wasn't willing to think about the stone. Not now. Not when he was about to put the animal-at-large in his proper place. Let the stone stay where it is, he thought. He'd deal with it when he'd finished the task at hand. He had lots of things awaiting his attention once he was finished, one of which was to look for a job. He'd been jobless for four months, ever since the evening when the owner of the accessory shop had fired him, saying, 'Find somewhere else to look for what you're looking for.'

That was all he'd said. Then Hashem had understood everything. He'd understood the secret behind the shop owner's surprise visits, and the close watch the other sales personnel had been keeping on him. Yet in spite of everything, he'd enjoyed the time he spent there, and he might not find another job like it. His former boss might even have turned other shop owners against him. But he'd keep looking until he found something.

He breathed in the air, which was redolent with the fragrance of farms and the smell of burning palm trunks. It had been a long day, but it had passed. Once he and Ayman had carried out their plan and he'd gone home, would his anger subside? Would silence dog him on the way back? What would he think about? And why should he think? He'd been thinking for too long already. There wasn't anything he hadn't thought about. New ideas might come, but what was the hurry? He'd think about those when their time came. For now, there was nothing but the streets of Medina, which came into view one after another as he tore down the road in his car, waiting to hunt down the animal that had hovered around a trap which looked like a sanctuary and . . . fallen into it.

Jubar ★ the 13th of Wail,
the twelfth year after Desert Storm
2 a.m., the Bab al-Tammar neighborhood

He heard the cracking of bones, and suddenly realized that he didn't want him to die. He pushed Ayman away from him, saying, 'That's enough! If you keep on this way, he's going to die!'

Ayman extricated himself from his grip, saying, 'So let the dog die, then.'

He pushed him farther away this time and grabbed the stick out of his hand, screaming, 'Enough! Enough!'

The heavy stone became hot, and heavier than before. All his strength left him, giving way to fear. He knew now what awaited him. He knew Musa's fate wasn't far from him. Why had he assumed that he was immune to such a fate?

He didn't want to turn to see the beaten body again. But he did turn. When he took a good look at Malek's body for the first time, he discovered to his pained surprise that there was nothing wrong with him. He wished he'd discovered some defect in him – any defect. But all he saw was a humble aspiration being buried without a shroud. Everything seemed still as death as the cool, pallid evening glow enveloped everything in sight. With difficulty he shuffled over to the body and stood near its head. He bent down and, placing his hands under the body's armpits, began pulling it away from the sidewalk toward the entrance of the building. Then he took off hurriedly in the direction of the car that stood parked nearby.

He placed his hands under Malek's armpits, and if he had brought them up to his nostrils now he could have smelled his odor. If he had, he might have realized that there was nothing to warrant the trouble he'd gone to.

This was the last thought he could remember. After that he didn't know what or who he'd thought about. The image of the blood-spattered body lying motionless on the sidewalk had forced all the other details out of his head. He wished he could get away from them, but he was dragging something heavy behind him: his mother, his sister, his father, the life he'd lived before and would never live again, the things he'd thought awaited him only to discover that he was the one who would go on waiting for them although they might never come; and death, the death whose nearness he'd fled from, the death that had waited for him, guffawing shamelessly, on a back street of Medina.

'Get in,' he said to Ayman.

But how did he know that the person he and Ayman had left behind wallowing in his blood had actually ridden his sister? Oh, God! Things had seemed so real just an hour earlier! But now, all the things he'd thought about were nothing but impressions and apprehensions that had been passing through his mind.

He saw everything shunning him as he drove away. Everything was moving backward, fleeing from him: the buildings, the trees, the lamp posts, the neon signs, and the strings of lights. Everything was moving away from him, leaving him with nothing but silence and death. For years he'd been running away from silence and death, yet now he suddenly realized that they'd always been in front of him. He'd been running in the belief that he was moving away from them. Little did he know that they would be waiting for him, there at the very moment when he thought he'd escaped from them.

4

The scent of sorrow

. . . According to statements published yesterday, Mohamed ElBaradei, Director-General of the International Atomic Energy Agency, said there is still nothing to indicate that Iraq possesses banned weapons. However, he added that more work will need to be done in order to confirm this. In an interview with Egypt's *Ahram* newspaper, ElBaradei said, 'There is no evidence thus far that these installations have undergone any change since 1998,' in a reference to the year in which searches for Iraqi weapons of mass destruction came to a halt. However, ElBaradei added, 'This needs to be confirmed. Inspections are still in their beginning stages.'

Munis ★ *the 15th of Wail,*
the twelfth year after Desert Storm
4:30 a.m., her room

Leen shrank into her chair as she saw her universe, whose details she had worked so diligently to arrange every night, fall apart before her very eyes without her being able to do a thing. She couldn't even cry. The only thing she could think about was Malek's face at the Dar Al Iman InterContinental with his unkempt sideburns and his somber handsomeness. She thought about the fact that she'd never told him what a special touch those unkempt sideburns added to his face. She couldn't say exactly what that 'special touch' was, but it was enchanting.

What harm would it have done for her to tell him that? If she'd kissed him, she would have known what they felt like. But she hadn't kissed him. She'd shut herself up alone in the bathroom and cried. Now her brother was telling her that he'd beaten him and that he might be dead, and she couldn't even cry.

She'd said to Malek, 'If you don't want to hurt me, you mustn't die.'

How could he die now without having told her that he was going to die? He'd called her at noon on the day of the beating, but he hadn't told her he was going to die! They'd talked a bit and he'd told her he was going to approach her father again about the matter of marriage. And, as always, he said to her, 'Take care of yourself.'

Then he'd said goodbye. But she hadn't said, 'Take care of yourself,' since she never said that to him. And even if she had, would that have kept him from dying?

Death!

She'd seen death numerous times. It had always come to her from its own place of safety. Death had no need to arrange its appointments. So how had she thought that Malek would call her just to inform her that he was going to die today or tomorrow, or that he'd died the day before, but hadn't had a chance to tell her until today?!

Oh my God.

She saw her father's face and remembered that she was in her room. She didn't know when Hashem had left the room, or when her mother had followed him out. However, she could make out the sound of her mother's weeping and mumbling. And she herself, why wasn't she weeping?

'Leen, are you all right?'

She looked into her father's face and saw everything he'd told her before. Had she done something wrong by loving a black man? Had she sinned against God or others? She'd loved a human being. She'd loved a heart of gold. She hadn't looked at his color. But her brother had looked at nothing *but* his color, and then he'd punished her for it.

Her father had said to her, 'People will never look at anything but his color, and they'll punish you, and I don't want you to suffer.'

Little had her father known that her brother would be the first one to punish her. Little had she known. The right half of her head had begun to throb. Time after time she'd complained to Malek about the migraine headaches that would come over her. He'd told her to stop hurting herself. But she hadn't hurt herself. She'd been hurt by others.

'Leen?'

She noticed her father's tone of voice, and could tell he was worried to death. She looked at him, wishing her face wouldn't betray what was churning deep inside her. She turned off the computer she'd been working at, then lay down on her bed and pulled her blanket over her. She felt a vague chill enveloping her heart, and when her eyes met her father's, she said, 'Dad, I want to sleep for a while.'

He knew she wouldn't sleep. He also knew she wouldn't talk. So, after turning off the lights in the room, he withdrew quietly and shut the door behind him.

The darkness was so merciful when it brought Malek to her. She saw his face in the shadows that had flooded her room. She saw his finely drawn eyebrows. She saw his wide, slightly yellowed eyes with their thick, curved lashes. She saw his broad nose, his thick lips, and the deep scar that had been left on his chin by an old wound, and that had always captivated her. It was so-o-o-o-o-o deep, she could have stretched out and fallen fast asleep inside it without anyone waking her up, saying, 'You're disturbing the dead. Find somewhere else to lie down.'

Was it necessary for her to think of him as a lifeless corpse on a back street of Medina in order for her to realize that her love for him had just been buried for a while under an accumulation of sorrow, but that it hadn't died? Had it been necessary for someone to murder him in order for her to know that love was alive and well, pulsating deep inside her, and that she'd just lost the way to it?

How long ago had she stopped telling him she loved him? And why had she stopped? Something deep inside had grown

lukewarm from the time he'd surprised her with the story of
'the absolution', as he referred to the Saudi citizenship he so
coveted. Her enthusiasm had waned. Her affection and longing had ebbed. She'd fallen ill, and hadn't recovered quickly.
Then the shock came to make her realize the heinousness of
her surrender. That's right. She'd surrendered to the silence
that had stretched out wide and cold between the two of
them. She'd surrendered to the birds of caution as they pecked
at the heads of her words, driving them back into their hiding
places. She had surrendered to the growing distance between
them. And she hadn't been able to resist a painful feeling that
he had let her down.

He'd called her often since mid-Sha'ban. He'd asked about
her and told her that he loved her and missed her. He'd told
her that he missed the two of them laughing together and
talking about the world and its filth. He longed to see her go
back to the way she'd been before, since he was the same as
he had been before. He longed for her to try – just try – to
forgive. But she hadn't gone back to the way she had been
before, and she hadn't forgiven.

She'd gone on talking to him half-heartedly, and even
when he broached the subject of marriage with her father, she
hadn't felt happy. She was going through with it out of duty,
plain and simple. She'd convinced herself that she wanted to
marry him for the sake of what was past, not for the sake of
what was to come. She'd been true to everything that had
developed between them, and only in this way had she
managed to accept the idea of a formal bond between them.
It seemed strange to her that they had such different motives
for wanting to make their relationship official. He wanted it
so that they could be together the way he'd always dreamed

of, and she wanted it so that everything that was past would have some meaning, since nothing that was to come mattered to her anymore. What was to come wasn't hers any longer. She'd refused to let him touch her at the Dar Al Iman InterContinental, and that had been enough to convince her that something deep inside her was amiss. It wasn't the way it had been before, and it might never be again.

Oh, God . . .

How had she thought about this while failing to notice that death can expose and rectify what, under ordinary circumstances, are the most rigid, obstinate, vainglorious of ideas? Death shook her up every time it came. And now, in the darkness of her room, she saw that she might never recover from the terrible realization of how cruel and foolish she had been.

Ever since mid-Sha'ban she'd been thinking about what her brother Hashem might do. She hadn't told Malek that her brother had seen her getting out of the pale blue Camry, or that she'd found him searching through her things and reading the letters they'd exchanged over the past few years. She hadn't even thought of telling him. And why should she have? She'd expected Hashem to take his anger out on her alone. But her intelligence had betrayed her. She'd lost sight of the fact that her brother was a coward who wouldn't have the guts to confront her directly, and that he would look for the most twisted possible way to 'discipline' her (read: hurt her).

If only Hashem knew that he had not only hurt her, but had devastated her to the point where she couldn't even cry anymore. Her eyes were dry, her heart was wracked with grief, and her spirit was full of yearning and distress as she prayed, 'Look at me, Lord! I beseech you, God, deliver me

43

from the state I'm in! Remove this heavy burden from me, and protect me from the evil that lies in wait for me – the evil of losing my faith in Your justice. Take my hand, God.'

She closed her eyes, but the darkness had already taken up residence in her spirit. She felt the force of the throbbing in the right side of her head, and when her stomach began to churn, she realized that the migraine coming on was going to be a terrible one. However, it wouldn't be any more terrible than the death that, as always, had come upon her unawares.

Shiyar ★ the 17th of Wail,
the twelfth year after Desert Storm
7 p.m., the hospital

Is he going to die?!

She kept pacing, agitated, up and down the corridor. His head bowed, her father sat on a white chair saying *la hawla wa la quwwata illa billah* as she walked anxiously in and out of the room. It hadn't occurred to him to get her out of the hospital for fear that she might lose her mind before his very eyes. She would have lost her mind if she hadn't come here, and her whole life would have collapsed. Every time her father had come to the hospital over the course of the past two days, he had refused to go into the room where Malek lay. She glimpsed a tremendous sorrow in his eyes. She didn't realize that he was terrified of her response, terrified of the moment when she realized there was no hope.

There's no hope. I've gone to hell.

It was hell for her to see Malek slumbering in a world she couldn't imagine. Why were they saying he was in a coma? He wasn't in a coma. He was just sleeping from exhaustion, and as soon as he'd had enough rest, he would open his eyes. All she had to do was sit on the edge of his bed and wait for his return so that she could show him the way back to himself. Meanwhile, her father sat on a cold white chair, waiting and praying that she wouldn't lose her mind.

45

Leen, Leen, L-e-e-e-e-n! What a beautiful name you have! How did your father manage to choose it? Leen, Leen . . .

But her name had died from the time when Malek had stopped calling her by it. His name had died, too, and it would be shrouded in this white coma. Who said comas were white? Who said comas had a color? Color! Color! Color, what have you done?

Is he going to die?

The doctor hurt her as he squeezed her wrist, shouting, 'Stop panicking!'

She looked at him gloomily and said, 'But you didn't know him!'

She came rushing in to see him, to touch him. She saw them taking the dead from corridor to corridor. She was agonized by the thought that they were going to take him, too, to some place from which there was no return, to a place where he would become a little mound hedged in by black stones. She thought back to the little mounds that had spread out before her eyes as she peered through the Baqi' Cemetery's Eastern Gate one day. Lined up in rows side by side, they were separated by snaking pathways. There was nothing but a cryptic silence broken by the sounds of the cars behind her. That day, after seeing how people end up, she'd thought she would be able to endure any tragedy that might come her way. But the waiting and the uncertainty had devastated her: the waiting for him to wake up, and the uncertainty as to whether he ever would.

When she saw Malek that morning, he seemed to be asleep. She nudged him gently, saying, 'Wake up. You've got a long day ahead of you!'

But he went on sleeping, and didn't smile. She gazed pensively at his gauze-wrapped head and his body enclosed in splints. His right leg, his right shoulder blade and two of his ribs were broken. He was on the verge of death, but he hadn't died. It horrified her to think that anyone would have the power to inflict this kind of harm on anyone – anyone at all! It horrified her even more to think that the person who had inflicted the harm was her own brother. She'd seen his violent side, but had never believed it would reach this extreme.

She went back to studying Malek again. She studied the scar that plunged so deeply into the flesh of his chin. She'd fallen in love with that scar, and many times had prayed to God that the children she bore him would inherit it. When she told him this, he had a long laugh, and asked, 'How could they inherit something I wasn't born with?' Nevertheless, she'd always thought of that scar as being imprinted on one of his genes, and that she had reason to hope. She placed her forefinger inside the scar's deep hollow. The moment she did it, she choked on her tears as she whispered, 'O merciful God, let me die, or let me wake up from this nightmare!'

She wiped her tears, then went back to pondering his still, expressionless face. It looked devoid of all meaning, as though it had been extracted from one of the dissection manuals she'd often looked at as she searched through the university library in the course of her studies. She remembered the Arabic translation of the *Sobotta Atlas of Human Anatomy* with its mustard-yellow cover and its reddish-brown title, and all the explanatory photos and drawings that filled its three volumes.

Dead people. Dead people's bodies and faces.

As she leafed through the volumes, she knew they were dead by the way their eyes had been drawn and the positions they were in. Dead people who'd been dissected slowly and deliberately, layer after layer after layer. First the skin had been stripped

47

away so that the muscles could be drawn. How beautiful and symmetrical they were! Then the muscles were removed so that the deep fascia beneath them could be drawn. The deep fascia looked supple, moist and slippery. And at last there appeared the bones, white and glossy. On the way to the bones, these dead people's skin, muscles, glands, veins, arteries and nerves had been removed slowly and carefully in order to reveal the bones' white blades and cylinders with their various sizes.

Bones, bones, bones. How bones had fascinated her! The thing that fascinated her most was dissecting the human skull. She would always recall the appearance of the three sutures drawn on the human skull: the coronal suture, the squamous suture and the lambdoid suture. Never, since the first time she'd seen them, had she been able to look at anyone's head without thinking of rivers: tortuous rivers on the surface of the skull. Two of these rivers – the coronal and lambdoid sutures – are parallel, one of them at the top of the skull and the other at its base, while the third – the squamous suture – runs between them midway along each side of the skull. Sometimes she would take her fingertips and try to feel the places where the rivers in her skull ran, and even though she'd never managed to do it, she kept trying.

She loved God with a passion after seeing those sutures. She loved a God who would cause three rivers to flow over a cranium. She smiled when she thought about the satellite photographs that have been taken of rivers on Earth, since there was no difference between the rivers on Earth and the rivers on the human skull.

Oh, God.

How had Malek's blank face made her think about three rivers on a skull? She studied him for a bit, then reached out

48

and placed her hand on his face. She let her index finger slide gently over the place where his palate bone was located: 'the lizard's body', as it was referred to in the *Sobotta Atlas*. She knew she was touching the spot over his parotid gland, right below the ear. Then she passed over the condylar process. Finally she paused near the mandibular foramen. Meanwhile, Malek was slumbering, oblivious to the rivers atop his cranium, the two openings at either end of his jaw, and the blood that flowed through his jugular vein and his sciatic artery. He was oblivious to everything, and she alone sat before him, removing the skin, the muscles, the fascia, the veins and the arteries from his cranium in order to stand on the banks of its three rivers. She hoped against hope that he would wake up – just wake up – even if he didn't know her, the one who had known him to the point of sorrow.

She was terrified of his dying, of his turning into a corpse like the ones she'd seen when a friend of hers had insisted on taking her to the autopsy room at King Abdulaziz University's Faculty of Medicine. There had been nothing but death there: faces submerged in a long, l-o-o-o-o-n-g slumber, and washed in medical solutions that would slow down their rate of decay. Decay, decay, decay!

The decay might be retarded, but it was bound to happen. She'd been trying for years to escape it. But when she'd gone to the autopsy room that day, she'd suddenly realized how weary she was of resisting it. She came to this realization as she was pondering the lifeless body of an unnamed little boy. According to her friend, a student had managed to facilitate his purchase from a man who worked at a certain hospital morgue. The six-year-old boy had been brutally raped and had been dead on arrival. He stayed in the morgue for months without being identified by anyone. Then . . . he was sold.

'My God, how could raucous laughter and hilarity have turned into a lifeless corpse that's changed color from all the time it's spent in a refrigerator? And how is it that no one identified him?'

'Maybe his family was afraid of a scandal,' her friend replied.

She felt as though he'd died two grievous deaths. She couldn't bear to look at his face, so she just looked at his plump little fingers and the black filth under his long fingernails. How strange, she thought, for a person to die, and for his fingernails to keep on growing!

She looked at Malek's fingernails. They weren't long. It occurred to her to trim them from time to time to keep them from getting long. It's only the dead who don't have anybody to trim their fingernails for them. But he wasn't dead. No, he wasn't dead.

8 p.m., the hospital
One time Malek had said to her, 'You're really stubborn about your ideas.'

She smiled impishly, raising her eyebrows. He acknowledged that there was nothing wrong with being stubborn if there was something worth being stubborn about. However, it turned into something offensive when somebody was just being stubborn for the sake of being stubborn. All right. Why was she thinking about her stubbornness now, in this room that was so unfamiliar to both of them, with Malek slumbering in his place of in-between-ness? What *should* she think about? About the first time he met her, weary and self-conscious, in order to tell her, 'I love you'? When had that been?

Oh, God.

She'd been an insomniac for long nights after that. It had seemed strange to her to sense everything that was developing deep inside him, to feel the words teetering on his lips every time he called her, yet without his saying them, and to see herself giving him time to say what was on his mind. She would deliberately prolong their conversations, invent reasons for him to call her again, or do other silly little things that she was puzzled to see herself doing, simply because she sensed what was going on inside him.

She'd supposed that, as soon as he finally said 'I love you', she would smile and lean back into her chair. But she hadn't. The spoken words had seemed different than they had in her imagination, and when they became a reality, she, too, became someone different from the person that had existed in her imagination – a person who wasn't able to smile or lean back in the chair. All her limbs went cold, and she felt as though her neck was paralyzed. When she looked into his face, she knew for certain that he hadn't slept for several nights, and that he'd resisted for a long time before speaking. Then at long last he'd sat across from her and said, 'I love you, Leen. I've tried, but I can't stand to keep it to myself any longer. There isn't anything around me any more that doesn't remind me of you. A couple of days ago I thought about you when I was stopped in front of a traffic light. I think about you all the time, actually, but when I was in front of that traffic light, I remembered your laugh. Why? I don't know. In any case, I didn't notice that the light had turned green, and I didn't hear the cars behind me honking. Imagine! I swear to God, I wasn't on Planet Earth. I was in some other place I don't know anything about. I'd been completely ignorant of it until

I met you. Would you believe it? I've started running away from people, from everything, so that I can be alone with you. I feel as though life is making fun of me. You know why? Because I used to make fun of love as it's described by lovers in movies, soap operas and Arabic songs. And now here I am, doing and saying the things they do and say. So, make fun of me, Leen. Go ahead. Mock me. Maybe God will punish you and you'll love me back!'

She bowed her head, suddenly gripped by loneliness – how she hated that feeling – and all sorts of sensations and thoughts began churning deep inside her. But nothing frightened her as much as feeling suspended alone in the heart of a storm. She remembered how, a few days after that evening, she'd looked into his eyes for a second, and in them she had glimpsed every moment she had ever passed through alone: the moment she'd stood atop the remains of Bab al-Majidi as bulldozers plied the site; the moment she'd received her high-school diploma; the moment when, looking out through the window of a Boeing 747, she'd glimpsed the lights on Airport Road as the airplane took off with her for Jeddah where she would begin her studies at King Abdulaziz University; the moment she'd first walked into the girls' dormitory; the moment she'd surrendered to a peculiar fit of weeping on the night before January 17, 1991; the moment she was told that her grand-mother had passed away; the moment she'd stood with her classmates, decked out in a graduation sash and smiling even though she was thinking about her grandmother buried in the ground and wondering what remained of her after all those years; and the moment she'd seen Sharaf's body being consumed by flames, so paralyzed by the shock at what she was seeing that she hadn't done a thing.

She'd lived through every one of those moments — and many others as well — alone, without there being anyone nearby to talk to about them. She hadn't wanted anyone to tell her that what she felt was good or bad. She'd wanted to be heard, but she'd never been able to get the words to come out. It terrified her to think of anyone — anyone at all — knowing of the turmoil she experienced in the face of her feelings and the vulnerability they left in their wake. Consequently, she'd resisted to the point where she was convinced that she didn't need to tell anyone what was going on inside her.

She was disconcerted when he asked her, 'Are you looking in my eyes to see whether I'm sincere?'

She felt the blood rushing hot to her face and her ears. It always upset her for her agitation to announce itself so rudely. She'd often wished she knew how to put on a poker face.

'It seems I've laid something heavy on you. You don't have to do anything but be yourself, Leen. I have a lot of things I'd like to say to you before you say yes or . . . no.'

She only smiled lest the situation turn into a dramatic scene. When she told him about this later, he laughed, and said he hadn't noticed. She found it fascinating to observe his nervousness, his little gestures, his way of pronouncing words, and the way he would alternately look at her and away from her.

'Please say whatever's on your mind,' she replied calmly.

'Thank you.'

She felt a slight pang inside when she heard him say, 'Thank you.' She didn't want him to feel indebted to her. She thought they should be equals from the start. There shouldn't be one party that gave and the other that felt indebted. She believed he was entitled to have her hear and understand what he had to say.

So she said abruptly, 'Don't thank me. I haven't said my piece yet. Later you might regret having thanked me!'

He went pale for a moment. But then he smiled, saying, 'Ever since I met you I've known you were a rare bird.'

Smiling back, she said, 'I can't stay long. But I'll be expecting a call from you.'

She got up and walked away, leaving him at the table in the coffee shop on the ground floor of the Sheraton without turning to look back. As she made her way to the front entrance she heard the sound of her footsteps on the marble corridor. She thought she was dreaming, that she hadn't met him, and that he hadn't said what he had said. But the scent of his tobacco and his cologne filled her nostrils and followed her all the way to the car.

He loves me!

She was encompassed by a worrisome silence, and the steeds of fear went galloping furiously through her deepest parts. She wasn't afraid of love but, rather, of herself. She knew she wouldn't be content to love him in the torpid shadow of the hypocrisy and incongruity that enveloped life around her. Time after time she'd tried to escape from them, and from the seething indignation she met with because she didn't accept without question what other people considered right, even though she had never once attempted to change their lives. No, she'd never made any idealistic attempt to change life. All she'd done was try to escape with all that she herself believed in. And now her escape was leading her to her death. Her relationship with Malek would expose the imperfection of life beneath her country's sky. It would tear the lustrous, silken fabric in which this putrid life had enrobed itself. And no one would forgive her. From the moment when she bade Malek farewell that day, she had realized that if she proceeded along love's rugged path, she would have to pay the price twice: once because she'd rent the veil, and once because she was a woman.

11 p.m., her room

When her father had come to the hospital that dawn, he hadn't said anything in particular. He had remained silent the entire time. Once or twice she'd caught glimpses of him squeezing the edge of his chair and trying to avoid looking her in the eye. She hadn't said anything, since she didn't suppose words would be of any help to him, but for his sake she had resisted falling apart. That was the least she could do, she thought. Then she realized that she loved her father not simply because he was her father, but because he loved her in this different sort of way, and because he didn't just claim to understand, but lived that understanding. It pained her to think that for days now, her father had been the victim of a bitter struggle between his love for her and what her brother Hashem had done.

Her father had come in to check on her twice since her return from the hospital. The first time, he had come cautiously up to the bed, hoping she would be asleep. As soon as he saw the light stealing in through the window reflected in her open eyes, he bowed his head, then left the room without saying anything.

'Dad,' she said, 'don't be sad. I won't lose my mind, and I won't die.'

But he had quietly pulled the door shut without hearing what she said. Fifteen minutes later he came back, so she closed her eyes on his account so that he would calm down somewhat and go to sleep. As soon as she heard the sound of the door closing behind him, she opened her eyes to the semi-darkness. Then she turned on a lamp to the right of her bed, whispering, 'Isn't there hope?'

Why didn't she sleep? How long had it been since she had slept?

'*O God of the heavens, sleep, a little sleep . . .*'

She laid her head on the pillow and began pondering the shadow her body cast on the wall in front of her, certain that she wouldn't go to sleep. She thought about the fact that Malek might have woken up, but with her far away from him. He might have been alarmed by the room's blue beds and walls. Everything in his room was blue: the walls, the blankets, the pillows, even the sky peeking in through the windowpane. Blue, blue, blue. Death is blue. The cloth that had been draped over the coffin they'd shipped her grandmother's body in from Jeddah, where she had died, to Medina many years earlier had been blue. When, after her grandmother's body had been removed for burial, the coffin had been opened for the last time, it had been empty like a blue, cloudless sky. She'd found out that when people die, they turn blue, then dry up. She closed her eyes, but she saw Malek alone, shrouded in blueness and hooked up to machines and tubes, and it pained her to think that he'd always been weary and alone.

Sighing dejectedly, she gazed at the color of the designs on her cotton shirt in the yellow light emanating from the lamp. She remembered the color of Malek's body in the same type of light, and the memory broke her heart. She could have scratched the color a bit, causing the layer of gold underneath it to glitter under that same light. It was a gold that had been smelted by untold interwoven sorrows, then forged and cast into a big, compassionate heart. How could she have failed to say such words to him before? How could she have failed to tell him about all her troubled little thoughts? She remembered his smile. She shut her eyes tightly. But how could she escape from what was there deep inside her? All the tricks she resorted to in an effort to flee led to the same deep pit, and she was afraid of what was inside it. She was afraid to look down into it and see the solitary, savage little girl concealed there. Malek had been capable of taming that little girl. And now she could almost see her — the little girl — becoming agitated in the darkness: blind, unkempt, fearful, wild.

Never for a moment had it occurred to her that things would turn out the way they had. But now she understood that her life had changed once and for all. She wished she could open her eyes and find herself napping on a chair in the semi-darkness, with a television screen in front of her flashing the images of WMD inspectors in Baghdad driving their white Land Cruisers from building to building, of Palestinian martyrs being escorted to their graves to the sound of ululations and loud shouts of '*Allahu akbar!* God is greatest!', and of George W. Bush inciting the civilized world against the 'axis of evil'. But that wasn't possible anymore. Everything that was past had been her own protracted dream. And now she'd woken up to the ugliness of people and things around her.

As she looked into Malek's face that evening, she knew she was trying not to cry, because if she did, she wouldn't be able to stop, and crying would take everything out of her. She also didn't want to cry because he might open his eyes all of a sudden, and it wouldn't be good for her to greet him with tears. But was he really going to open his eyes? If he didn't, all their memories would quickly vanish. They would fade as though they'd been left in the hot sun. They would lose their features and their colors. They would wilt before anyone had taken notice of them, like the little bushes that had been planted up and down Al Jamiat Road. Once as she and Malek were driving past them she'd said to him, 'How can they neglect such a marvelous thing?'

With a smile he'd replied, 'And who else would think about things the way you do?'

As she passed her hand over his head that evening, she prayed to God that if the angels approached him, they would only approach to bring him back to life. She saw a wild deer running through grassy meadows. She smelled the odor of its dung. She smelled the odor of the bed's cold metal. She smelled the odor of Malek's body. At the right corner of his mouth she saw a small patch of congealed blood. She took a paper tissue out of a packet next to her and cautiously began scratching it off with her fingernails. When it had all come off, she placed it gently on the tissue in front of her. Then she carefully wrapped it up and deposited it in her purse's inner pocket.

Why had she done that? She didn't know. What was she going to do with a clump of congealed blood – put it with his pictures, letters and gifts? Would this be the last thing that remained to her from him – a clump of congealed blood that was sure to go to pieces?

She closed her eyes. But that wasn't going to protect her from her thoughts.

*The beginning of the 18th of Wail,
the twelfth year after Desert Storm
1:30 a.m., her room*

The next day her father would tell her, 'You've got to stop visiting him.' And she wouldn't be able to say, 'I can't.'

He'd done what no other man would have done, and she didn't want to put any more pressure on him. She'd seen how agonized he was as she stood before him in tears in the hospital lobby. 'Dad,' she begged, 'all I want to do is make sure he's all right! I know I've been completely out of line. But I'm about to suffocate, Dad. I'm about to go crazy. And I'll go even crazier if I keep thinking how my brother is the person who did this to him and I haven't tried to visit him. Dad, please. You know what kind of man Malek is. Don't be unfair to him the way Hashem was. And don't be unfair to me. Please, Dad!'

With a mournful expression etched on his face, her father kept repeating, *la hawla wa la quwwata illa billah* and *hasbi Allah wa ni'm al-wakil.* For a moment she realized how difficult she was being. But then she thought to herself that after all, he was her father, and he'd put up with all her foolishness. At the very least, he wouldn't slap her and curse the day she came into his life.

Placing his hand on her shoulder, he said, 'Calm down, Leen.' Then he took her to the wound-dressing room. He was so distraught, he didn't know how to turn on the lights.

However, he managed to get her over to a bed in the midst of her sobs.

'Calm down, Leen. Calm down.'

She tried to calm down for his sake. She wasn't sure whether he would agree to let her stay at the hospital near Malek or not. She was weary, and hadn't slept a wink for some time. A few moments later her father came back with a nurse. Speaking broken Arabic, he asked her to help Leen.

The nurse replied with a smile, 'Not worry, Baba. God willing she all right. I give her medicine for sleep.'

The nurse brought her a glass of water and a pill which she placed in her hand with a collusive wink. Feeling grateful for the nurse's complicity, she popped it into her mouth. Then she gulped down a little water as the nurse began spreading a blanket over her legs. Not long afterwards she saw her father leave the room and heard him muttering across the corridor. Staring into the darkness, she prayed, 'O merciful God, look upon me. Let Your mercy rain down on me. Let me wake up from this nightmare. O merciful God, if You aren't angry with me, send down Your mercy onto my spirit. Send down Your peace, O God of the heavens.'

At some point she drifted off, but she woke up, alarmed, to the sound of her parents' voices rising in the darkness. Where was she? No sooner had she gotten her bearings than the door flung open and she saw her mother standing in front of her. She heard her voice ringing out, 'I obviously didn't know how to raise you! Aren't you ashamed of yourself? Do you want us to be the talk of the town?'

She hadn't been dreaming, then. Her father really had left her at the hospital. And her mother? Her mother, who had given birth to her, was standing before her unable to show her any compassion. Leen made no reply. She kept her head bowed, her eyes fixed on the reflection of the light coming from outside onto the room's dull tile floor. After sending away some nurses and a doctor or two who'd come running to find out what was going on, her father came inside and closed the door behind him.

With muffled rage he said to her mother, 'We didn't come here for you to raise your voice!'

'You don't want me to raise my voice? If you'd raised your daughter right, maybe I wouldn't be raising my voice!'

Then, turning to Leen, she said, 'God damn you, you smarty pants! I'd rather have died than had you! You come along with me right now!'

Grabbing Leen by the wrist, she began tugging on her. However, Leen wrested her hand violently from her mother's grip. Taking a step backward, she said breathlessly, 'I'm not leaving the hospital. Do whatever you think is best. You can even stay with me. But I'm not leaving here.'

The rage pent up from all the years past had begun flowing in her veins. It was the rage of a ten-year-old girl who'd come to an early awareness that she wasn't wanted but didn't understand why, the isolation that had confined her spirit, the loneliness that had sapped her, the neglect, the disregard, and the belittlement of everything she'd ever accomplished in her life. For more than twenty years she hadn't meant a thing to her mother. So how could her mother expect to drag her away by the arm now, just like that, as though she were still a little girl, or as though nothing and nobody had changed?

Her father bowed his head, while her mother continued to eye her, her breathing rapid as she struggled to keep her rage and bewilderment in check. Leen didn't know how to remind her mother that she was her daughter, and that people would never stop looking down on her no matter what she did. They would always find some excuse to despise her and talk about her behind her back, while her mother, with her screaming and carrying on, had given them all the more reason to do so. She thought of going over and kissing her on the forehead, but she knew her mother would callously push her away, and she didn't want to make her pain all the worse. She was tired, and all she wanted to do was to wash her face in cold water, hoping – and not for the last time – to discover that everything that had happened was nothing but a long, long nightmare, and that she just didn't know anymore how to wake up from it.

Gazing into her mother's angry face, she said to her forlornly, 'Wake up, Mom. You must be dreaming. What happens to me and what I do is of no concern to you. It was never of any concern to you in the past, so why should I believe it's of concern to you now? You're not even worried about me. (*God, have mercy.*) You're only worried about Hashem. But believe it or not, Mom, I won't say a thing. Are you afraid I might talk? I won't. And I assure you that when Malek wakes up, he won't talk, either. So don't worry. Trust me, if only just this once. Go to Hashem and tell him, "They won't do anything to hurt you. They wouldn't do that. Everything will be forgotten." Now go away and leave me alone. I don't want anybody here anymore. I don't want anybody anymore.'

She ran to the door and opened it awkwardly, then took off in search of a bathroom where she could wash her face. When she came back, they were gone. The door of the room was open, and the scent of sorrow emanated from its every corner. But does sorrow have a scent?

3 a.m., her room

She remembered walking distractedly through the hospital lobby two nights earlier in search of Malek. Her search hadn't lasted long. She'd requested a taxi in the wee hours of the morning and left the house without saying a word to anyone. She sat in the back seat feeling sad, bewildered, angry and apprehensive. Strangely, she'd felt happy because she'd learned that, although his condition wasn't stable, he hadn't died. When she called his house, his brother Yusuf had answered. She'd paid no attention to his wary, surprised tone of voice. She'd wanted to know what had happened to Malek, and was prepared to let Yusuf think whatever he wanted to. Suspicions had steadily eaten away at her spirit. She didn't ask him for any details. She simply asked about Malek. When Yusuf told her he was in the hospital in a coma, she sat down on the edge of the bed. Before calling to ask about him that night, she'd spent hours standing in front of the window, and she'd wept as she watched the morning approach with sluggish breaths. Standing at her window, she'd thought she would never see him again. She'd summoned an image of his face and nearly burst into tears. She hadn't seen his face since the day they'd met at the Dar Al Iman InterContinental, and her longings confused her. Did she miss him because she'd been uncompassionate toward both him and the two of them on that day? Or did she miss him because she knew that even if she saw him, she wouldn't find him – he wouldn't be there? He would be far, far away, like a star on whose points the tattered remains of her dreams now hung, and she would wait patiently without being distracted by anything, even sleep.

O God, is there no sleep to be had?

She wasn't going to fall asleep. She turned toward the other side of the bed as even the tiniest details of her grief kept coming to mind.

She loved him. She really did. However, the issue had to do not with love, but, rather, with the way people around her looked at this love, the way people in her country would deal with a love that had torn through the transparent partition that was raised like a protective barrier between different colors, races and ethnicities when it came to love and marriage.

In the beginning she and Malek had stood on opposite sides of this transparent barrier. He'd spread his hand on it from one side, and she'd spread hers on the other. There hadn't been any warmth. They'd been right up against each other, so she would rest her head on his chest under his right collarbone, but he couldn't put his arms around her and feel the contours of her body. With a growing exasperation she'd dug her fingernails into the meadow of his chest from behind the unseen wall. Then suddenly, part of the see-through partition between them had torn right between his left collarbone and his heart. Quietly and cautiously, she'd started widening the hole until she managed finally to cross over and touch him. Every time they met, she would pass through the hole and touch him.

And how she'd loved to touch him.

She'd loved to let her hand roam through the grass on his chest as they talked. They would talk a little about themselves and what awaited them, and a lot about life and its problems, about Al Ittihad, the people's football team and Al Hilal, the government team, about the crossword puzzles she'd collected in her desk drawer so that they could solve them together some early morning, and about Taher Katalouj's songs. He would sing them to her, which made her laugh and love him even more.

Every time her hand went roaming through the grass on his chest, she would glimpse a little deer grazing along the edges. It was a pale sandy color, its eyes wide and glistening with little white windows lined up inside them, and it would peer out at a horizon she didn't recognize. It was a lone deer in an open expanse without a hunter in sight. Did the deer love him? How happy she must be! After all, the aspect of their love that might cause the gazelle pain was the part that was past, not the part that was yet to come. The deer could go on grazing on the grass on his chest despite the white splint, and when he opened his eyes, she would be the first to know.

Leen closed her eyes. But what good would that do?

Everything they'd ever said and done lay hidden in the deep darkness of her spirit. She recalled the first time he'd ever called her. She'd been leafing through files stacked on her desk when the telephone rang, and he'd been on the other end. He'd told her he was writing a newspaper report on runaway girls, and that he hoped she would help him given the nature of her work at the Social Welfare Home. There'd been nothing strange about such a call, and it hadn't even occurred to her to ask him how he'd gotten her number. That had been the beginning. Everything had begun from that point without their knowing it. As they talked, she'd noticed that his questions were different from other people's. They struck her as the questions of someone who tries not to dwell on outcomes because he wants to understand the causes.

They'd talked for a long time that day, and the following days as well. Later, when he told her how books had become his consolation, she'd known what it was that made him different.

When the report was published he called her to tell her, and they went back to talking like a couple of friends who'd been out of touch for a day or two. He expressed genuine sympathy for the girls, saying he believed that what drove them to run away was despair of finding any other way out. When she got up the courage to speak to him about the little notebook where she wrote down her observations about the girls and some of her conversations with them during their stay at the Home, she somehow knew that Malek was going to be more than just a passing acquaintance.

'Observations?' he asked in surprise.

'Yes,' she replied. 'Little thoughts.'

'About all the cases?'

'No, only the most striking ones, the ones that leave me speechless, and that force me to stop and think.'

'I think that's part of the beauty of your work.'

'It's also part of what makes it unpleasant.'

Quite some time later he had asked her in passing, 'Leen, do you remember the notebook you talked to me about, where you write down your observations about the runaway girls?'

'What about it?'

'Would it be possible for me to look at it?'

'But . . .'

'But what?'

'It would be sort of embarrassing for me to let you read my thoughts. I'd feel pretty exposed.'

'I'd hate you to feel that way with me.'

'I didn't mean . . . it's just that I wrote things down the way I felt them, and I'm afraid you might hear a shrill voice that isn't really saying anything.'

'Have a little faith in me, and let me be the judge of that.'

'You're going to find a lot of grief,' she said, and sighed.

'I can take it,' he said calmly. 'Through it I'll know how to get through to your spirit.'

Her spirit?

Her spirit was so tattered, you could see through the holes in it to the emptiness deep inside, where there was nothing but her enervating sense of having been let down. It had kept getting emptier and emptier and emptier until it started to rob her of sleep.

She opened her desk drawer and took out the notebook. Then she started leafing through its pages and reading . . .

. . . When they brought her to the Home for the first time, she was recovering from her illness. She was short, emaciated and jaundiced, and her narrow forehead was covered with fine wrinkles. Her papers said she was from Badiyat al-Shallahah and that she was fifteen years old. If I'd seen her outside the Home, I would have thought she was a lot older than that. Muznah didn't say a word the entire time, and the following morning the supervisor told me she'd spent the night sobbing miserably.

When she sat down on the chair in front of me, she said, 'I'm sick.'

'I know. I sensed that yesterday.'

She didn't look up from the floor. Fearfully she asked, 'Are you going to send me back? I don't want to go back.'

'Why not, Muznah?'

'It hurts me.'

I didn't understand. 'Does it hurt you to go back to your family?' I asked stupidly.

But she didn't reply. She remained silent, wandering about in a realm I knew nothing about. I felt slightly ashamed as I looked at her cracked hands. Seeing what a rough life she'd had, I hid my own hands. By the time I finished reading her file, I knew how much pain she must be in. I knew she had probably been raped. However, I knew he was her husband, and I realized who and what she meant when she said, 'It hurts me.'

How trivial things seemed then. My whole life seemed trivial. I thought about how, when I cry, I cry over trivial things, and how, when I get sad, I get sad over trivial things. I also thought about how I hold my life in my own hands. No one's taken it away from me. I haven't lost it yet. And, though I don't know why, I thought about the fact that Muznah is aware of her pain, but she doesn't understand it the way I do. For a fleeting moment I had the certainty that Muznah would never realize the seriousness of her loss. When she ran away, she'd been running away from pain. She'd wanted not to hurt. But she would never be aware of the injustice she'd endured – or at least, she wouldn't be aware of it in the way I was. And she would go on believing, possibly till her dying day, that her father had married her off because this is what fathers do when their daughters grow up. They marry them off to the first suitor that strikes their fancy. And 'Awad had struck her father's fancy. Besides, he was his paternal cousin, he lived in Medina, he'd paid a handsome dowry, and he'd bought her father a new minivan. He might even have been older than her father. But age doesn't diminish a man. There's nothing that can diminish a man. Her father hadn't made a mistake when he gave her in marriage. It was just that she hadn't been able to bear the pain. She'd tried, but the pain had just gotten worse. By the third day she realized she wouldn't be able to take any more, and she had no one to turn to. So she ran away.

She said she knew that if she went home, her father would send her back to her husband, so she'd decided to run away to the streets and squares near the sacred mosque. It was from there that she'd been brought to the hospital in a pathetic state. When the physician examined her, he suspected that she had been raped. Consequently, she'd been referred to the Social Welfare Home, where she'd begun to talk and everything became clear.

What are they going to do for her? Nothing to speak of. They'll summon her father or her husband, and whoever comes will sign a pledge not to do her harm. Then he'll receive her and take her away. She won't have the option of saying no. She'll cry, but no one has the authority to keep her at the Home as long as she's fifteen years old and has family members who are willing to take her.

'It hurts me . . .'

She looked up from the notebook, and for a moment she kept repeating the words, 'It hurts me, it hurts me, it hurts me.'

But – she wondered as she leafed through the pages of the notebook again – was it pain she was feeling? She scanned quickly down the page until she came to the name 'Sharaf', and stopped up short. The ugly creature hidden inside a tiny box jumped out. It had a foul odor. For a moment she felt on the verge of nausea. She remembered how she'd gone on feeling nauseous for days after Sharaf's death, and how she hadn't been able to get rid of the smell of burned hair. The smell of it had clung even to her skin despite the fact that, during the days that followed the event, she'd bathed over and over again. She'd cried for a long time in the shower, remembering the body in flames passing before her eyes. Meanwhile, a voice uttering words she couldn't make out echoed everywhere like an evil omen. The voice replied to her questions in a way that both bewildered and fascinated her. She kept wondering how a marvelous creature like Sharaf could die. How could she have surrendered to despair that way?

'. . . And he danced with me.'

I stared at her for a moment, amazed. 'Did you need somebody to dance with you?'

'What I needed was to be alive. When I met him, I knew how dead I'd been.'

'Is he the one who taught you how to put words together this way?'

She smiled with resignation, saying, 'No. I'd been afflicted with words before I knew him. I left notebooks filled with words in my family's house, and I think they found them and tore them up. One time he told me my words weren't bad even though they described bad things.'

'What bad things?'

'The bad things in my life.'

'Is your life bad?'

'Look at where I am now.'

'And was your running away going to take you to a life that wasn't bad?'

'I didn't run away.'

'So, then . . .?'

'I left a house where I wasn't able to find an iota of understanding.'

'You left?'

'Yeah. Just the way you leave your home every morning to go to work.'

'But I come back again.'

'As for me, I can't go back to pain anymore.'

'Has what you did freed you from pain?'

She smiled dolefully. 'How can you speak to me in that tone of voice? What do you know about pain?'

'I know enough about it for you to trust me. I've suffered, too.'

'No! You don't know what I know about pain. You've never been beaten by a younger brother because you hadn't made the tea for him and his friends. You've never had to keep yourself from blowing up while you ask him, "What right do you have to beat me?" only to have your mother scold you, saying, "Sh–sh–sh–sh. Don't raise your voice at your brother!" You don't know what it's like to have your brother force you out of the car when you're about to go with your mother on a family visit. He doesn't explain why he's insisting that you get out and not go with your mother. All he does is say coldly, "You're not going anywhere. Come on, get out!" Then at midnight he suddenly opens the door to your room and says, "That's so you won't get out of line again, and when I tell you to do something, you'll do it and keep your mouth shut." Then he slams the door. No. You don't know what pain is. And you don't know what humiliation is. I was nothing but an object in that house. I wasn't a living creature. How could I have done anything but leave?'

'But you took a huge risk for the sake of a man you hardly know.'

'Maybe. But I'd been suffering for so long, I'd started to turn savage. I didn't want to turn any more savage. I ran away so that I wouldn't lose what was left of my life. I wanted to marry him, but they wouldn't let me.'

'Why?'

'He doesn't have "an absolution".'

She said it with bitter sarcasm. Then she went on, 'I ran away so that I could marry him in court. The clerics there looked suspiciously at me, and one of them sent me away. He said, "Go get your guardian, girl." "You're my guardian, Sir," I told him. "I would be," he grumbled, "if the man you want to marry were a Saudi." That made me mad. I said, "But he's Arab and Muslim." "Don't talk so much," he told me rudely. "Bring your legal guardian and a paper from the Ministry of the Interior. Then God will solve your problem for you . . ."'

But Sharaf didn't wait until God could solve her problem for her. Instead she delivered her body to the flames, leaving the odor of her incinerated hair clinging to everything and everyone she passed. And Leen – when she saw the flaming body rushing past her – what had she done? Nothing. Nothing at all. She'd just stood there, her neck paralyzed with fear, and all her physical strength gone. She couldn't turn, scream, or run after her to help her. She'd seen the supervisors and some of the girls racing by, and she'd heard people screaming and calling out. She'd seen panic and tears. She'd seen a woman throw a blanket over the body and fling it to the ground. As for her, all she'd done was stand at a distance. Sinking into her deep, dark depths, she'd been pulled inward with blind force, and was helpless to understand why. She couldn't even imagine how despair could be so dreadful.

4 a.m., her room

From the moment she glimpsed Hashem's face that night, she knew he'd pulled one of his innumerable stupid pranks, but she hadn't thought it had anything to do with her. When their eyes met, she saw a look she didn't know how to understand or interpret at the time. He was frightened and agitated. So she, too, became frightened. Something had happened, but she didn't want to think about its being something bad. Bad things don't happen this quickly. She saw her mother splashing water on his face and wiping his head with it as she recited Suras 112, 113 and 114 of the Qur'an to ward off the evil she dreaded. At that moment the two of them looked to her the way they always did: like a couple of Siamese twins fused back to belly. Her mother was always behind him: protecting him, pushing him, directing him along life's intersecting paths. At moments like these, all Leen could feel was that she was a mere happenstance, and, sometimes, a drain on their existence. Their existence was complete. Hence, there was no need for her to be a part of it, or even to check in with them from time to time. Hashem avoided looking at her as he rushed to his room with her mother close on his heels. If she'd taken a long look into his eyes, she would have seen Malek lying there, bleeding and in pain. But she didn't.

73

Hashem!

Oh, God! How many years had passed since her mother gave birth to him?

Her mother had been about to wither up like an old palm branch, and would have done so if she hadn't given birth to him. Her uterus had been unstable, and her fetuses were weak and vulnerable. No sooner had they begun to develop than they would lose their hold on the uterine wall, leaving her with nothing but heartbreak, sorrow, and an increasingly fierce desire to try again. She'd cried for a long time before her body swelled up in a frightening way, with her belly hanging down in front of her like a huge, solid pumpkin. And she was happy. She did nothing but lie around and relax lest her unborn child get angry and leave her the way others had. She would caress her belly, and when the baby began to kick, she would take Leen's hand and place it on its outer wall. At those moments she would have a captivating expression on her face, perhaps because she was so happy. Life had taught her – belatedly, as usual – that happiness is like magic, because it makes a person beautiful.

Malek had often said, 'All you lack is joy.'

Her mother hadn't just been happy. She'd been like someone who was about to produce a miracle that would eventually reveal itself as a crime.

For long nights prior to this she had cried, asking her husband, 'Isn't God ever going to give me a son? I want support from my children. I don't want to die among strangers. I want a son who'll take care of me when I get sick and old. But Leen isn't ours.'

Leen had tried to understand why she wasn't enough for her mother, why she didn't bring her the joy she expected to receive from the male she longed for. But she'd never been able to figure it out. Every Friday afternoon before conceiving Hashem, her mother would take her by the hand and they would walk down the narrow streets of Bab al-Majidi neighborhood – in the days when there'd been a neighborhood by that name – to the holy precincts. They would go in by the 'Uthman Gate. Once there, her mother would withdraw to an out-of-the-way spot where she would perform ritual prayers and offer supplications, and sometimes she would break down and weep. Leen would busy herself throwing grain to the pigeons that came fluttering down one after another into the mosque's open-air courtyard paved with gravel and sand. Every now and then she would glance over at her mother, then at the men on the other side of the court-yard as they came to perform the sundown prayer. Life at that time hadn't been marred yet, and the holy precincts were still without partitions, screens or men with long beards and gruff voices who would shout at those coming in, 'Hey, let's go, *hajji*! This is a women's area. The men's section is over there.' As they spoke, they might jostle an elderly man leaning on a cane who knew only enough Arabic to recite the Fatihah in his ritual prayers.

Those had been the good old days, although, as far as her mother was concerned, they hadn't been fruitful ones. So she'd kept on repeating her prayers and supplications while making regular visits to women she'd been told might be able to help her. Looking back, Leen realized how hard it had been on both her and her mother. She remembered going with her mother one day to the house of one of those women. As she waited outside under an almond tree, its untrimmed branches hanging down about her, she'd looked for a

75

cloudless sky where she could shout, 'O Lord, give my mother what she wants!'

And He'd done it. Her body had ballooned in an alarming way, filled with a secret sap that nearly concealed her eyes beneath mounds of flesh that were soft and supple to the touch. It also caused a few freckles to appear on her neck and cheeks and raised the level of albumen in her body. But because she was so happy, she was beautiful.

She still remembered how happy her mother had been as she bought diapers and baby clothes, and how certain she'd been that she was carrying a boy. She only spoke of the baby as 'he' or 'him', and her entire life was changing on account of this little one who'd taken so long to appear. Her mother had believed he would survive, so he did, and when she came home from the hospital carrying him in her arms, her face radiated an overwhelming joy. Bringing him up close to Leen, she'd said, 'Kiss the head of your protector.'

Oh my God, how ludicrous that word sounds now!

She hadn't said anything, and she hadn't come up close to him. She just stared at him as he stretched in her mother's arms. Then she said, 'Why is he so red? He smells funny.'

Her mother smiled as she breathed him in. 'Yes,' she said. 'He smells sweet.'

Her mother had named him Hashem, and kept him at a distance from life. She doted on him, banishing Leen from the circle that enclosed the two of them. This had grieved her immensely, because at the tender young age of ten she'd been incapable of either comprehending or excusing.

Once Hashem appeared in her mother's world, her life came to rest on three foundations: his health, his demands and his mood. The minute any of these three was shaken, her universe would turn upside down, and the sky would change its color. Birds no longer had names, people no longer had faces, hope lost its meaning, and God in His heaven was no longer merciful as she'd thought Him to be. When her baby got sick – and he would always be her 'baby' – she would lift her eyes to the heavens and say reproachfully, 'Why, Lord? He's the only one I've got!'

Then she would cry. She would cry if he got sick, and cry if he got well. She would cry if he cried, and cry if he smiled. She would cry if he left, and cry if he came home. She would cry if he spoke, and cry if he said nothing. She would cry because before he arrived, her life had been empty, and cry because after he'd arrived, it had gotten overcrowded with his details and his little things. She was afraid he would abandon her, leaving her with a life that had been devoid of him twice: once before he had come, and once after he had come.

In the past Leen had thought about her mother. She'd loved her, but she hadn't understood her, and the ability to understand is sometimes more important than love. Now she did understand her, and she had something to protect her from desolation, something to protect her from the belief that her mother had deliberately neglected her. But now it was too late. She'd stopped blaming her. However, she couldn't forgive, because she'd always believed that children are God's gift and that they don't choose to be female or male, and perhaps because she'd realized early on that she was better than him. But the fact that she was female had been an unforgivable sin.

Yet in spite of all her pain, her mother was still her mother, and Hashem was still her mother's Hashem: her first and last dream, the unborn child before whose arrival she'd knocked on so many doors. He was still both her dread and her refuge, the key that had opened the gates of women's paradise for her. She'd once been Selma, and was now 'Umm Hashem' – Mother of Hashem. The tongues that had wagged behind her back, labeling her 'poor thing', had been cut off. She now had someone on whose life, whose nearness, whose absence and whose presence she could swear – though never once had she sworn by his death. Her existence had at last been validated, and it no longer mattered to her whether she conceived again. So she made no more efforts to do so, being content now with her Hashem.

Leen watched her mother float on the water of life, weightless as a feather. She was beside herself with delight as she watched Hashem grow. She watched the little boy open up to reveal the teenager within. She watched the teenager open up to reveal the young man within. However, what was revealed wasn't always good, since her pampering had spoiled him. Then his limited intelligence had taken care of the rest, spoiling both his life and hers.

Leen found herself thinking about how her life had been ruined by an inept, worthless child, certain that it would never be the same again. Nothing and no one would go back to what they had been before Hashem's act of folly: not her mother, not her father, not she, not Malek. Indeed, Hashem himself would never be the same again. She thought about how discomfited he'd been when he saw her, his panic attacks at night, his burning desire to flee. She wished she could see the horrific nightmares that filled his nights, tormenting him and driving him out of the house, the nightmares that had caused him to speak unconsciously and reveal what he had done. She wished she could know the words that hovered at the edges of his throat when he saw her. They choked him and forced him to run away from her, leaving her with nothing but sorrow and helplessness.

She wished she'd said to him, 'Take it easy. I may blame you for a while, but some day I'll stop. It isn't your fault. You're nothing but the pathetic echo of a voice that's even more pathetic.'

She'd tried to say it on a couple of occasions, but when she found herself unable to get the words out, she'd stopped trying. The wound was still fresh, still oozing pain and sorrow, and it would be a long time before its scab dried up and she could scratch it without hurting all over again.

Now she was conjuring her brother's features. She was sure it would be a long time before she knew which, of the many feelings churning inside her, she would experience from then on whenever she saw his face. Which feeling would cling to her spirit? Sadness? Rage? Pain? A sense of betrayal? Bitterness? She bowed her head as she suddenly realized that none of the emotions keeping her spirit in such turmoil would bring Malek back. Not even her brother's remorse could do that.

She closed her eyes and realized that, as she attempted to make sense of what had happened, she was a spirit that had suddenly been emptied of its joy. From then on she would have fish eyes: lifeless eyes that rotate in their sockets without betraying the slightest warmth or intimacy. If she wanted to die now, she could do so without worrying about leaving him behind, since he was no longer either behind her or in front of her. She no longer knew where he was, or even where she was, for that matter.

She could die now, because she wasn't going to live anymore, and might not even try to. When he told her about the 'absolution', she had died a little. However, she hadn't died so completely that she couldn't revive again when something shook her powerfully. This 'something' had caused her to wake up before her spirit escaped from her. Now, though, she knew she would close her heavy door tight and hear the bolt sliding along its track. That would be the last sound that connected her to life, the life she wished she had known how to live without being blamed or having war waged on her most of the time.

But . . . there wasn't any more life for her to live. There was nothing but a vast desolation. Even if she were given another life, it wouldn't be enough to enable her to lift him up again. Her spirit was so tattered, how could she mend its holes all over again now that everything she'd counted on had seeped out through them? Who and what would protect her now from the secret desperation that was spreading like a stubborn oil stain on a piece of untreated red silk? It was bound to shrink if it was washed, and rubbing it would ruin it. Its color might fade a bit, and every time she looked at it she would go on seeing the spot. Besides, she wondered, can anybody wash despair out of his or her heart?

How stupid she was!

How could she have thought that others would make peace with her way of thinking if she couldn't impose it on them? How could she have thought that the confrontation would be easy? On what basis had she assumed that she was different from Muznah, Ayisha, Reem or any of the other girls whose papers had crossed her desk at the Home? How could she have thought that she was immune to a fate like Sharaf's? Why had she believed that her fate was in her own hands, that her life belonged to her and that no one would take it away from her? Now, in pained surprise, she'd become aware of the fact that fates can be similar even if the paths that lead us toward them are different, and that her life could, indeed, be taken away from her regardless of how different she seemed from these other women and girls.

Different?

What would have led her to believe that she was different from the other females around her?

Was she different because, if she wanted to, she could drive a car without her father objecting?

Was she different because she'd managed to get her own ID card?

Was she different because she traveled without an escort?

Was she different because her cell phone and most of her other belongings were registered in her own name rather than that of her father or her brother?

Was she different because she . . .?

Was she different because she . . .?

But now she saw all these things as tenuous and tainted, like sawdust floating on the surface of stagnant, putrid water. Now, belatedly, she knew her true size, and she knew what she had to be. She knew the boundary she wasn't to cross, and that she mustn't allow others to cross.

4:30 a.m., her room

She thought about how Malek's spirit must be roaming the heavens bewildered at that moment, and how everything she was feeling stood between her and the possibility of bringing that spirit back. She thought about how, if she was distracted momentarily, his spirit would pass through the tunnel and there really *would* be no hope. She was terrified. Her life had been tied to him even in its minutest details, and she'd loved him so intensely that she'd never once thought that part of her life would pass without him.

When she saw him the next morning she would wipe his face with her perfume. She would tell him she wished she could have stayed with him, but that the things standing between them were things that other people considered to be more sacred than what God has spoken from His heaven, that they would hurt her father, and that she didn't want anybody to hurt her father. He'd been a good father for as long as she could remember, and she knew he would go on being a good father as long as she lived. He would put up with whatever silly things she might do or say in the future, and would never hate her. He might hate what she was doing, or what she had done. He might wish to himself that he'd fathered her in some other time and place. But it wouldn't be because he hated her. On the contrary, it would be because he loved her. Yes, he loved her. And all she had to do was calm down.

'*Calm down, Leen. Calm down. And take refuge in the water.*'

She pulled back her blanket, opened her wardrobe and took out the first thing she came to. She hadn't brought a towel with her, but that wasn't important. She went to the bathroom, where her body trembled slightly before she stepped under the cold water that gushed out of the showerhead.

'*Water – what an incredible blessing: a molecule of oxygen and two molecules of hydrogen, and you have water, and tears.*'

She stood there under the gushing water, contemplating it as it descended in straight, spoke-like lines, then broke over the contours of her body before slipping out through the small metal drain. As it descended, it took with it the pain that had been pulsating for two whole days through her right temple, the joints of her feet and the four chambers of her heart. She heard the pain whirl down the drain, then gurgle through the inner pipes as the dawn call to prayer reached her through the little glass window to her right.

Oh, God!

She closed her eyes beneath the flow of water, recollecting everything that was past: the long years the two of them had known together, the letters they'd exchanged, the names they'd cursed, the tears she'd shed, the anger, the coffee, the packet of Halwani semolina cakes he'd brought her once, the feeling that used to come over her whenever a light-blue car drove by, the dreams whose details she would ponder after waking, imploring God not to let them give way to pain, and the times when she'd been gripped by an overwhelming longing for him only to have her phone ring at that very moment and bring her his voice:

'I was asleep, and I dreamed you were calling out to me.'

All she could do at those times was surrender to silence, awed by love's ability to make her spirit so light that, like a feather, it could caress his heart and bring him to her.

Before long the dawn light would be spreading abroad and the city streets would be bustling with life. In the meantime, Malek was still slumbering in his place of in-between-ness. It would be some time before he awoke, and when he did, she would be far away from him, and changed. Her spirit had changed.

Hot tears streamed noiselessly down, and she was swallowed up by a terrible feeling of loneliness and lostness. She remembered all the nights she'd spent gazing up at the distant sky with its stars suspended in space – at the times when it was possible to see them. They would gleam with a mysteriousness that gave her a sense of her insignificance and the insignificance of her sorrows. During those nights she would wonder how a past suspended in a distant sky could so defeat her. How could a star that had gleamed millions of years before – and that, for all she knew, might still exist, or might have turned into a black hole – make her life, her whole life, into such a trivial thing?

And now, how would her life appear? And would she be able to bear what this life was to become? Did anything await her? She realized that she had to sharpen her mind so as to preserve for him the image of the life in which he was no longer present so that, if he came back, he wouldn't be shaken through and through by confusion. They would have the stuff of a long conversation. And when they had their conversation, she would cry. Yes, she would cry the way she was crying now, though not as miserably. She would tell him she'd learned what Hell is, and that she'd pleaded with God not to cast her into it twice.

5

The absolution

The movement in opposition to the war on Iraq is gaining daily momentum in US universities, particularly among on-campus residents, although professors and students do not expect protests to reach their peak until the war is actually underway. Student protests against the possible war are concentrated in New York University and Hunter College. However, some observers believe that the students who are apathetic about the issue still outnumber the activists who are losing sleep over the possible outbreak of this conflict. Some analysts have stated that as hundreds of students rush to Washington DC to demonstrate their opposition to the anticipated war, thousands of others are likely to stay where they are until the first military strike has been launched.

Dubar ★ the 24th of Adhil,
the twelfth year after Desert Storm

'I know I'm late in saying this, and that you might blame me when I do say it. However, saying it isn't going to change anything.'

'. . .'

'I'm almost sure it's never crossed your mind, and that it won't mean anything to you. Excuse me. I'm stumbling over my words. I just don't know where to start.'

'From the beginning. Say what you have to say in the fewest, clearest words possible.'

'I haven't received an "absolution".'

He said it in a tone that he attempted to make sound disdainful, and a chill blew up. The telephone remained suspended, motionless, between her shoulder and her ear. Her eyes fixed on a painting on the wall before her, she saw the clouds in the picture move apart, their notched edges looking like demons standing in a long line between her and him. For a fleeting moment she suspected that God in His heaven had stepped between them, and the world disappeared from view behind leaden shadows of hopelessness and heartache.

An absolution, an absolution, an absolution.

Where had she heard it before? Where, when, and how? From beneath which mound had this derisive tone emerged, and the guffaw that now filled the empty space in her head?

A vulgar, shameless guffaw, it reminded her of the titters of the girls at the university cafeteria, something that might issue from someone who's overly repressed, but not from a normal, healthy human being.

Oh, God.

How many clouds had traversed the city's autumn sky, suspended, like the telephone, between earth and heaven? How many prayers had left the holy precincts for the Lote tree that marks the end of the seventh heaven? How many spirits had opened the portals to the world of the unseen in those moments, running after the steed of knowledge only to have the steed kick them, then wink and escape with a smile?

He said nothing. She said nothing. They were hemmed in by a heavy, stifling, alarming silence. When she finally managed to discern something of her surroundings, she saw them stealing into her room from all directions: from under the door, through the window, through the air-conditioner vent, through the electrical outlets. She saw everyone who, before long, would discover that she had punctured the sacred, transparent barrier they'd erected ages ago to keep colors, races and ethnic groups from mingling, and as a result of which corruption had taken up residence in both land and sea. They filled the room and, with sardonic smiles, said one after the other, 'We told you he was a *takruni*, but you didn't get it. Now you've ended up with another disaster on your hands, and you're the last to know.'

The killer phrase had been the final one: '. . . the last to know.'

For so long she'd thought she was close to him. And now, what should she find but that she was farther away from him than she could ever have imagined? Pain crushed her ribs, and something in her heart was torn to pieces. She thought about how Malek had had a part in causing this pain, and a part of her heart was torn to pieces. A little part that swore never to forgive him.

'Why are you so quiet? Say something. Tell me off. Tell me you're angry, that I'm a bastard and that I don't even deserve for you to listen to me anymore.'

'You had no right to hide something like this from me.'

'I wasn't hiding it. I didn't think it would mean anything to you.'

'What you thought was a dangerous thing, and what you did was even more dangerous!'

'What do you mean, Leen? Don't scare me, and don't be cruel to me.'

'You were cruel before I was. You'll never know what you've done.'

'. . .'

'You've hurt me, and you've hurt yourself. And I don't think I'll ever be able to forgive you.'

'But . . . maybe you're right. Maybe I shouldn't have kept something like this from you. There were moments when I thought of telling you. But I didn't want to upset you. I've been trying for the last two years to get my status changed. Throughout this time I've dreamed of being able to tell you about it in the past tense. I thought I'd be granted citizenship soon, and that once that had happened, it wouldn't be a bad thing for me to tell you that I was born here, but was only recently granted a certificate sealed with two swords uprooting a palm tree. Try to understand my motives. They weren't bad at all.'

'And you, didn't you ever think about the pain I'm feeling now? If I told you you'd deceived me, could you deny it or blame me? Look where you've put me in your life. I always thought I was close to you, really close. And now I come to find out that I'm far away. You forced me to pressure you mercilessly to tell me something that a lot of other people around you already knew – a lot of people who may not have any intimate ties to you. Malek, how many times did you talk to me about the dilemma you faced, and that was forcing you to postpone our engagement? How many times did I try to find out what kind of a dilemma you were talking about? But all you did was keep telling me it didn't concern me. You sat back and watched while I floundered about, worrying, racking my brain, not knowing what to think. I was about to doubt your intentions toward me. Yet none of that was enough to get you to take pity on me and tell me what your dilemma was.'

She'd once written to him, saying, 'I know the moment when I started to change.' As she hurriedly threw out these words of hers, she'd realized she was changing, although she hadn't known what she was changing into. The right half of her head was throbbing violently, and she wanted to end the call before she said something she would regret.

She saw the cosmos confining her behind a cold glass barrier. She could see and hear everything on the other side, but all she could feel was cold. Even Malek she saw beyond the barrier, and she didn't cry. Deep inside her there churned all the feelings that make a person want to cry, but without knowing how. Her throat went dry. Her spirit also seemed dry, as though love had never touched her.

With difficulty she said, 'I'd like to go now. I don't have anything to say, and there's nothing I want to hear.'

'Take it easy, Leen. I love you.'

'And you've proved it,' she said mockingly.

'Leen!' he cried at the same moment.

He couldn't see that she wasn't mocking him. She was mocking the innocence of hers that had so charmed him. Now she knew why it had charmed him. She was mocking the moment she'd once been so sure they would never have to face, only to find them facing it when they'd least expected to.

'Let me go before I hurt you with my words. I don't want to do that, and if I go on talking, it's bound to lead to pain.'

'Watch out, then, for the Leen I know, so that she won't hurt the Leen I love.'

Click . . . and she hung up. She didn't even wait for him to hang up first the way she always did. She went over to her wardrobe and brought out a medium-sized, colorful box that held his letters, the box that, long months later, she would find Hashem hunched over, rummaging through its contents and scattering her photos.

She began reading his letters and underlining the places where he had communicated respect for her difference, her mind, and her ability to understand:

I refused to get involved with women before I met you because I wanted a woman who was different: <u>a woman who would enthrall me with her mind</u> . . . They say that Muhammad 'Abd al-Jawwad is the most accomplished left-back in the history of Saudi soccer. They always like to use superlatives: the best, the most beautiful, etc.! They're free to do as they like, and I'm free to do as I like. So I say: <u>To me you're the most amazing woman</u> . . . A prostitute phoned me yesterday. She claimed she was from Riyadh. I almost weakened and went to her. <u>But I only remembered you</u>. So I didn't give in . . . <u>Would it surprise you if I told you that your love has taught me to swear off racism</u>? I used to be prone to it, horrible as it is. After all, there's nothing strange about that in a society that feeds us on its stereotypes from the time we're born: Indians are called *'rafig'*, Bedouins are called 'Serbs', Hejazis are called *'Tarsh Bahr'*, Egyptians are called swindlers, Lebanese are called pimps. And those are only some of the filthy epithets I used to use, but your love cleansed me of them.

She kept wondering: if he really saw her this way, then why had he concealed his dilemma from her? She was alarmed to see how his behavior had given the lie to all the words he'd written about her, about life, about what ought to be and what ought not to be. She'd believed in the silly principle that says people should live according to the way they think. She'd clashed with lots of people around her because of this naïve principle since it flew in the face of the prevailing way of life in her country: her country, where people said what they didn't do and did what they didn't say. Her country, where life was being destroyed by corrosion after spinning endlessly round and round in a stinking mire. Like a vast unpolished silver surface – rough, frigid, and massive – her country needed a little hellfire to melt it down, purify it and reshape it. But God hadn't sent down His punishment yet.

It alarmed her to see the way his behavior gave the lie to the romantic picture of love that had filled her mind and that she couldn't let go of. For a long time she'd thought that love meant being close to someone, as close as close could be. But suddenly she'd realized that, like anything else in life, love is subject to a person's particular ideas and way of life.

Even so, regardless of his motives or his way of life, Malek had had no right to conceal such a thing from her. After all, it didn't concern him alone, but both of them together. It concerned the relationship between them. She would always think of it this way, and she would go on wondering what had caused him to behave as he had. Had he been worried about how she might react if she knew? Had he been trying to spare her pain? And what pain? She wouldn't have been in pain. Rather, she would have understood the dilemma he faced and would have thought with him about how they could resolve it. She wouldn't have pressured him or hurt him. Nor would she have gotten caught up in waiting for a commitment she had thought was imminent only to find that it was far, far away. She would have understood. But he'd chosen for her not to understand, believing – as he always did – that he was sparing her harm, and that the matter didn't concern her despite the fact that it concerned her to the point of being excruciating.

Oh, God. So he didn't know me after all. All those telephone calls and all those times spent together suddenly show themselves to be flawed. All we were doing was wasting time on a long, drawn-out prattle.

She was filled with rage, bitterness, confusion, amazement and grief. When she began thinking about the fact that there might be other things he had concealed, was concealing, or would have concealed from her in the future, she realized, with difficulty, that she'd lost faith in him. And when she reached that moment, she came back to her old oyster shell, the one she'd opened for his sake, and let it quietly close around her. She stopped being happy: she stopped being the heavenly creature — as he used to call her — that had captivated him with its sweet spirit and pristine innocence. She stopped telling him she loved him or that she missed him, or that she was sad. Blame thrashed about deep inside her like a little child restrained to a bed. But she didn't want to blame him, since blame wouldn't do any good. It wouldn't give him an 'absolution', and it wouldn't restore order to the chaos his actions had left in their wake.

A few days later, she adamantly refused to see him. She knew now that she was angry, but she didn't know how to get rid of the anger, which had turned her into what he described as 'a poisoned blade thrust into my heart'. She didn't deny this, but she also didn't tell him that he was the one who had thrust the blade when he chose to relate to her as though they were starring in some sappy Arab film: the star conceals his big secret from his sweetheart in the belief that he's doing the right thing, which leads her to think badly of him. He revels in the role of victim until suddenly all the facts come out and she cries giddily, 'Do you really love me that much, Sharif?!' in response to which he nods his head with a smile before the words 'The End' descend on the screen over their heads. And, as the fairy tale goes, 'They lived happily ever after.' But life isn't like films, and that's part of the tragedy, since the other part is that in the rough-and-tumble of our everyday lives we forget all about films, and we don't forgive ourselves when we try to turn our long, tumultuous lives into quick flicks with happy endings.

She'd decided not to blame him and had struggled mightily not to do so. She might have succeeded in keeping herself from blaming him. However, she wasn't what she had been before. She couldn't fight off the wave of grief that had flooded over her heart and spirit. And Malek couldn't see any justification for that grief. Consequently, he was filled with a bitterness and resentment that he didn't understand. He thought the source of her grief was that she was resisting her desire to run away from him. He voiced this thought directly at times and alluded to it at others. But she said nothing. She didn't know how to make him understand that of all the feelings that had churned deep inside her – rage, resentment, confusion, amazement, and grief – grief was all that remained. All the other feelings were gone, and nothing was left but her old heartache. She didn't know how to make him understand how painful it was for her to watch her lifetime – which she'd wanted to spend with him – slip through her fingers like cold water. Her days were devoid of even the shadows of the gaiety whose time she had thought had come, only to see it dissipate like a fleeting summer cloud. Out of the blue she'd discovered something else that also prevented them from committing themselves to each other. Besides color, there were other, unyielding restrictions. There was another barrier they would have to breach in order to reach each other. She'd thought for a moment that everything was about to fall into place. However, a blind force had suddenly pulled her back without giving her a chance to realize what was happening to her. Nothing on earth pained her the way it did for things to come too late. This was a part of her that Malek hadn't understood. He'd tried, but he hadn't been able to comprehend the pain that wrung her heart. How could she rejoice in something whose presence would only remind her of the long, painful time she'd spent waiting for him? And how could he understand her spirit's anguish?

She was about to turn thirty – her old dream. She'd begun to explore whether it was possible for a woman to reach the age of thirty without a husband or young children in a country where a woman's existence was only validated by having a husband or a son. She'd been waiting anxiously for her thirtieth birthday. Never once had she met a woman in these desert sands who was waiting for her thirtieth birthday or even thinking about waiting for it. But turning thirty was her unique obsession. During her teen years she'd thought it must be a magical event for somebody – anybody – to become thirty years old. So she'd started waiting for it, and what a long wait it had seemed to be.

At fifteen, people waited to become twenty so that they could seem grown-up in the eyes of those around them. She thought back on the dreams suspended there in the lavender sky of twenty, the expanse that opened onto infinity, the rashness, the sweet frivolity, the forgivable imprudence, the naïve ideas that made people think life could never betray them, and the heart that never tired of searching for a special sorrow, since sorrow is maturity, and happy people and those who laugh a lot are gullible folks who don't know what life is about. As for the sorrowful, they're the mature ones. The sorrowful are the children of life. She'd thought about all this. Still, all she'd been waiting for was her thirtieth birthday. She had believed – though she didn't know why – that by the time she turned thirty she would have surmounted the obstacles in her life. And she thought she would reach that age with a heart that was still tender and glowing, a spirit that hadn't been broken, and wisdom that was still intact.

God, Leen! Where were you going to get wisdom thinking like that?

She scoffed at herself as she remembered how she had imagined that once she turned thirty, she would experience profound happiness: a staid, thoughtful happiness, not a frivolous, light-headed happiness. But does happiness wait a lifetime before it comes? And is it possible for someone to describe happiness as being 'staid and thoughtful' or 'frivolous and light-headed' without being scoffed at?

Ha, ha, ha! Laugh, Leen. Have a long laugh over your naïve ideas. Ha, ha, ha, ha, ha, ha, ha, ha, ha! Have a good long laugh that puts a miserable lump in your throat at the end of every 'ha' while the tears pour endlessly down. Ha, ha, ha. A person only turns thirty once. Ha, ha, ha. You've left thirty behind forever. You reached it once, Leen. Then you left it with a wizened heart, a tattered spirit, and no wisdom. Ha, ha, ha. Malek says, 'You're a flawless woman.' No, you're a woman who's nothing but flaws, nothing but flaws, nothing but fl-a-a-a-a-a-ws. Ha, ha, ha.

Thirty!

What she had done was far less than she'd always thought she would. By the time her mother turned thirty, she'd given birth to her daughter, and to her sacred male Hashem. And now, her mother would look at her with a sigh – sometimes – surrounded by her stacks of books and papers. For all she knew, her mother might be wondering what she'd done wrong to make her daughter turn out this way, and whether she would forever be stuck with books and words she didn't understand and didn't want to understand. She might be wondering what her daughter found in a world in which there was nothing but books stacked in neat rows atop the shelves or piled near her bed: a world of paper. Leen had never expected her mother to understand the secret that lay behind her attachment to a world that seemed suited not to a woman but to a man. When a man wastes his life on books, no one blames him. And the moment he comes to his senses (since books, like drugs, rob a person of his senses), life is there waiting for him. Life will always be waiting for the man, since he makes his life. As for the woman, she waits for hers. No matter how old he gets, a man can always start all over again. He's bound to find a woman and have children. And he'll find a woman and have children even if he remains attached to his books. As for the woman, well . . .

Oh, how a woman suffers!

And she had suffered. She'd suffered for a long time, certain that she had never been close to him in the past, and that she would never be close to him in the days to come. Depression hadn't been her preferred choice. She'd striven mightily to recover the spirit that had once been hers, but she found herself alone, with no one to support her. And Malek? It pained her to realize that his love was no longer a haven where she could find refuge when life took her by surprise. It pained her even more to think – if even for a moment – that most of her suffering now came from this very love. As she spread out its large fabric in front of her every night, trying to mend its holes, she wondered if he was there on the other end doing the same thing. It agonized her to see herself having turned into a cold, hopeless machine. She would wake up tired after a fitful sleep, read a little and work a lot. She would eat and drink because she had to. She'd grown thin, very thin, as she waited to recover from the loss of her first hope. And when she didn't recover, she promised herself not to let life torment her with hope ever again for fear that the wait might reveal something else she wouldn't be able to bear. The moments pierced her heart as she thought about the fact that they – that is, all the moments that were passing with Malek far away – would have been more pleasant if he were near. But nothing had ever brought him near: not the letters, not the phone calls, not the furtive trysts. Nothing had brought him near, and nothing ever would. At least not now, or tomorrow, or the day after that. It would be a long time before he was near, if it ever happened at all. She would always think this way. It might not be to his liking, but it was the only way she knew how to think, and after all her years of living, it wouldn't be possible for her to learn some other way. So, was she supposed to apologize for this? Should he blame her for shuttering hope's windows as she fled from any glimmer of hope – as she fled even from seeing him?

For months he'd pressed her to let him see her. After despairing of the idea, he'd stopped insisting. Then, a few days earlier, he'd called. A long year had nearly passed since she'd learned of the 'absolution'. It was mid-Sha'ban.

When he called her he said, 'I'm in the mood for a pre-Ramadan picnic. I'm in the mood for *mushabbak*, *hamam al-barr*, and you.'

She remained silent. Any word she might think of saying would open up like a fresh wound. When she finally gathered the courage to speak, she said in a tone that she hoped wouldn't betray her agitation, 'You don't get it.'

'I want to get it. But I'll never get it until I see you and we can talk. There isn't a single part of me that hasn't suffered,

Leen. You think you're the only one who's suffering. Pain has torn me to pieces, but I still have hope.'

'Hope!'

'That's right, even if it doesn't sit well with you. Maybe I don't understand why you don't want to let yourself hope, as you put it. But you also don't understand what it means to me to have hope where you're concerned. I gave up on hope once before I knew you, and I don't want to give up on it again. We should get together and talk so that we can know if we should swear off hope or hold onto it. Give it a try. You won't lose anything. We met often before, and it wouldn't be a bad thing for us to meet again.'

They were enveloped in a heavy silence. Then at last she said, 'I'll think about it.'

He smiled. She didn't see him smile, but she knew he had. The fact that she knew it amazed her. She didn't know if she would go to see him or not. However, she did know that if she went, she wouldn't be the Leen he'd known before, the Leen he was expecting. Maybe she was a bit afraid of what he would find. She wondered if he would love her with this sick, troubled spirit of hers. However, she didn't pause for long over the question. She was already thinking about their meeting: what would it be like after all this time? She was thinking about it as her cell phone flashed in the darkness of her room: Malek is calling, Malek is calling, Malek is calling. But she didn't answer. She didn't want to give in to the pressure he was putting on her. She wanted to go because she wanted to go, not because he wanted to see her.

In a cool room on the seventh floor of the Dar Al Iman InterContinental, they met for the first time in long months. When she looked into his face, she felt as though he'd suddenly grown old. He'd let his sideburns grow out, which made his face look a bit different, and handsome in a sorrowful sort of way. She went over to a window and looked out at the neon sign advertising the Al Ghazali Trading Company. It blinked on and off with agonizing monotony. Then she turned to him. He shot her a smile so sad it brought tears to her eyes. Anything at that moment could have brought tears to her eyes – even the doodles she noticed on a piece of paper he'd placed on a table.

When he reached out to touch her cheek, she instinctively pulled back. He knit his brow for a moment, but smiled forgivingly, since he understood that she hadn't meant to hurt him. She was in pain. He was in pain, too. And here they were meeting after all these months like a couple of old friends who'd run into each other at a station, unsuspecting and unprepared. They both had things to say, but they didn't know how to begin saying them or put their thoughts into words. They were traveling a secret, shared path in each other's direction, but they'd lost their way. For a moment she wished she could cry. He brought out a pack of Marlboro Lights, then lit a cigarette and began puffing away.

'O woman of the futile silence, is it not time for thy silence to be broken?'

She looked at him in some amazement, perhaps at his eloquence and the dramatic tone in which he had addressed her. Fiddling with her fingers, she said, 'I didn't come here to talk. I came to hear what you have to say.'

'You've changed.'

'I don't deny it. Is that what you wanted to say?'

He put out his cigarette and drew up close to her. Her body went tense, and she prayed to God that he wouldn't come any closer. He reached out and laid his hand on her left shoulder. He didn't seem to understand that she didn't want him to touch her – at least, not at that moment. She removed his hand quietly from her shoulder, then got up hurriedly and went to the bathroom. She shut the door behind her. Then, leaning against the door, she sat down on the cold floor and wept. The hum of the air coming out of the air-conditioning vent in the bathroom ceiling, the deadly silence concealed in everything, the smell of his cigarette smoke clinging to her clothes, and her certainty that he knew she was crying at that moment without knocking on the door to ask her what was wrong – all these things stood over her like terrifying mythical creatures. She saw the oyster shell closing around her and wished she could scream, 'Hurry! Catch me before it's too late!' She washed her face. The water was cold and her face was hot. Then she came out of the bathroom, got out her *abaya* which was hanging in a cupboard near the door, and put it on. When she turned to look at him, she found him sitting where he had been before, puffing away on his cigarette.

'I'll be going.'

'I'll give you a ride.'

'No. I'll go out to the street and look for a taxi.'

He looked at her for a few moments. Then he said imploringly, 'Don't be mean. Grant me this one little pleasure. Let me take you home. I'll let you out near the house. Don't say no. Please.'

So she didn't say no. The blue Camry glinted beneath the huge street lights along the new streets around the holy precincts, streets whose names she didn't know and didn't want to know. She felt as though they were alone in the midst of the congestion at the intersection of 60th and Abu Dharr

Street. She imagined the crowds of people inside the holy precincts and in its outer courtyards. She thought about how many of the people in the cars around them were either leaving the holy precincts or on their way there for a pre-Ramadan picnic. She remembered all the times when she, her mother and Hashem had put on new clothes and headed for the holy precincts to have a pre-Ramadan picnic with her mother's friends and their children. She remembered the heat that would emanate from the *mushabbak* as it melted in her mouth, the taste of the *hamam al-barr* that she loved, and the popcorn, and the *manfoush*. How long had it been since her mother had stopped going on pre-Ramadan picnics? And why had she stopped? How long had it been since the city had stopped being what she'd known and loved? She had memories of times and places that were no longer hers. Memories that were so far removed from what she saw now, she thought she must have just made them up in order to keep nostalgia from destroying her. But when had nostalgia destroyed anyone?

When she awoke from her reverie, Malek had pulled up in his Camry along the frontage road near where she lived.

He said, 'I'm not going to pressure you. I'll wait until you've gotten over your bad feelings. We'll meet again soon, right?'

She made no reply. She remained silent for a moment. Then she got out of the car and closed the door behind her. But the moment she turned to head home, she saw Hashem standing there on a corner nearby. He was just steps away from her, with a look on his face that unsettled her.

Time stood still for a few moments. During those moments Malek backed the car up a bit before taking off without noticing her brother Hashem. This, to her, was an answer to prayer, since she hadn't wanted anything to happen in the street.

Hashem said nothing when she passed him, and her chest tightened. There was something ominous behind the silence.

6

Decay

Iraq challenged the United States yesterday to show UN inspectors the information it claims to possess on banned Iraqi arms programs. 'Amer al-Sa'di, advisor to Iraqi President Saddam Hussein, stated in a press conference that Iraq hopes its declaration of its arms programs will meet with the approval of the United States because it is up-to-date, precise, comprehensive and truthful as required. Al-Sa'di added that if Washington has evidence that conflicts with this declaration, it should present it to the International Atomic Energy Agency or the UN Monitoring, Verification and Inspection Commission (UNMOVIC), noting that these bodies can verify the matter. Iraq has given UN inspectors a huge file of documents and information on its weapons programs and previous activities which, according to al-Sa'di, confirms that Iraq has no banned weapons in its possession.

Ahwan ★ *the 5th of Wail,*
the twelfth year after Desert Storm

He hadn't wanted life to break her. Yet now he found himself, not life, implicated in doing just that. He'd hoped his daughter would be different. However, this same hope now caused him pain. He'd suddenly realized how burdensome her difference was, and with all the love, fear and concern he felt, he wanted to tell her that nothing could compare with her being his daughter. But the words lodged in his gullet like a piece of dry bread. He gulped once, twice, three times. But the weary, sorrowful words refused to leave their places. He developed a miserable lump in his throat that nothing could take away.

He said to her, 'I can't, Leen. They'll hurt you, and I won't be able to bear it.'

'But I'll be able to bear it, Dad. They'll hurt me for a while, then get distracted with their own affairs.'

He took a long look at her. He looked into her eyes. In them he saw everything that life had withheld from him. He thought for a moment about how he'd never seen his mother, the result being that he couldn't be sure whether there was anything of her in his daughter: some characteristic feature or mannerism. But even if there'd been nothing of his mother in her, this wouldn't have made him love her any less.

As he looked at her, he wished he could tell her how much he loved her, and how much he'd loved her even before she was born. He wished he could tell her how his attention had been arrested by the fifth verse of Surat al-Hashr, which reads, 'Whatever of their palm trees you may have cut down, or left standing on their roots, was done by God's leave . . .' He wished he could tell her how he kept repeating to himself, *leena, leena, leena* – 'palm tree, palm tree, palm tree . . .' He'd read in *Lisan al-'Arab*,

> In the passage from the Divine Revelation, 'Whatever of their palm trees you may have cut down', the word rendered 'palm tree' (*leena*; plural *leen*) refers to every part of the tree with the exception of the dates themselves.

The idea flashed quickly through his mind, and he held onto it: he'd name his baby girl Leen. The name Leena seemed too common – not terribly common, but well-known and famil-iar. But the name Leen struck him as unique. He didn't want her to have a name that was hackneyed and worn-out. He didn't know why he had believed, at the time, that her name should be worthy of her, but he'd developed a growing certainty that she would be no ordinary human being. It was a certainty that had nothing to do with parents' pride and their overblown ideas about their children. No. If it had been that sort of thing, he would have known how to ignore it. Rather, it was a goal, and because it was a goal, he would achieve it. This is how he had thought, and this was what he had decided at that time. And now here he was, standing before her. He saw how the days had clothed his certainty with flesh, nerves and bones, and how they had given it a tongue with which to address him.

She stood before him in the grip of a silence saturated with reproach. He bowed his head, wondering how he could persuade her that he had been choosing her, not other people's approval, when he said no to Malek. With what words could he tell her that he saw what she didn't see, that he was aware of things she wasn't aware of, and that he was being no less courageous than she was when he had chosen to say no? For although the price of saying no might be exorbitant, the price of saying yes would have been more exorbitant still. If he'd said yes, he would have been opening the door to her misery with his own two hands, and he could never have stopped blaming himself whenever a shadow of torment or pain crossed her face.

Perhaps, if he'd loved her less, he would have said yes. But he couldn't. He just couldn't. Two nights had passed since Malek broached the subject with him, and all he could do was toss and turn. He could see clearly what would happen to his daughter if he said yes. She would be happy for a little while, and be in torment for long years to come. He knew people would never leave her in peace. They would tear her apart in his presence and in his absence alike. He'd also become increasingly convinced that people wouldn't be content with mere words. Rather, they would try to change what wasn't to their liking.

It dismayed him to think back on all the stories he'd heard in the course of his work at the court. He remembered the story of two young men who had abducted their paternal cousin and her husband by force and taken them deep into the Du'aythah region far from watchful eyes. Once there, they'd ordered the man at gunpoint to divorce their cousin. When he refused, they'd murdered him right in front of her. Then they fled, leaving her alone with her treacherously murdered husband. And why had they done this? Because her husband didn't belong to their tribe! He had spent many a sleepless night thinking about those two young men's paternal uncle — the young woman's father — who told the judge with bitter sobs how his daughter had been taken to a mental hospital in a state of collapse. He said that killing his brother's two sons wouldn't restore things to the way they had been, that they were his flesh and blood, and that he'd already lived through two tragedies and didn't want to cause a third.

It dismayed him even more to remember a white girl who had come to the court with her brother to be wed to a young black man her father had refused to allow her to marry. Some religious authorities at the court took her to a side room and began grilling her: 'Why do you want to marry a black?' 'Is he threatening to do something to you? If so, tell us, and we'll take care of it.' 'Have the two of you committed sexual immorality?'

God!

What would people do to his daughter if he said yes to Malek? What would the religious authorities at the court say to him?

'My goodness, Abu Hashem! Couldn't you find anybody but this slave to marry your daughter to? Has she gone bad so that no men want her anymore? If you'd only told us, we would have taken care of it. The country's full of eligible bachelors, Abu Hashem.'

Hashem?

What would Hashem do? He was sure to commit some folly no less cruel than what those two young men had done. Hashem disapproved of many things his sister had done. So how could he possibly approve of her marrying Malek? He might murder him, or murder her. He was hotheaded enough to do something like that. What would he say to the judge then? And what would he say to her? How could he protect her from herself? How could he persuade her that life wasn't a mirror image of her ideas?

He'd been close to her in the past, but he hadn't felt the need to protect her the way he did now. And he *would* protect her. He certainly would, even if he had to cause her pain in the process. She would suffer for a while, then recover. Her recovery might take a long time. Yet that would still be more merciful than losing her forever. She'd been given to him once, and never again would he have another daughter like her.

He thought back on the feeling that had come over him when the nurse brought him the happy news of her birth. God, it was as though it just happened yesterday. And today he suddenly realized that his daughter had turned thirty. Her grandmother had placed her in his arms and he'd recited the *adhan* in her right ear and the *iqama* in her left. As he did so, he'd been flooded with a wave of bliss that made him feel as though he were floating on air. Then he left Leen, her mother and her grandmother at the hospital and headed for the holy precincts. He felt he ought to say thank you to God for the gift He'd given him, and for her and her mother's wellbeing. As he made his way to the holy precincts, he thought about many moments in his life that had changed him or the world around him, and he sensed that the birth of his daughter had turned all the moments he had experienced in his youth, and which he had thought of as so incomparable, into ordinary moments that now retreated into the recesses of his memory: Gagarin's orbit around the Earth and the uproar that had attended it, King Saud's removal from power, the beginning of TV broadcasting, the first used car he'd ever bought, the

Saudi-Yemeni war, the Arabs' defeat in the 1967 Six-Day War, the Americans' landing on the moon, and his first airplane trip a few years before Leen was born. All these moments, and others as well, paled into insignificance when he first held her in his arms and felt the warmth of her tiny body.

On that day, when he passed the school for orphans at Bab al-Majidi, he sighed as he thought about how life, monumental as it is, is fragile, and how joy and sorrow prompt people to think about it in new ways that may cause them to rearrange its details all over again. He remembered the fear that had overtaken him as his wife went through labor behind closed doors. As he paced the corridor, anxiety chewed him up, then spit him out again, then chewed him up all over again. Every time the door opened and another stretcher came creaking through, he thought they'd brought his wife out. Nurses went in and out time after time without looking his way, but he couldn't bring himself to sit down, even for a little while, even though his bones were getting stiff. But all that fear had vanished the moment he took his little girl in his arms and breathed in her pristine aroma.

He had traveled life's roads alone for a long time before his daughter was born. When she was born, he felt there was hope that she might bring him some companionship. Once, many years earlier, as he was on his way to the holy precincts, he'd thought about this. He'd also thought about what life had in store for her. His life hadn't been an easy one, and when he bowed in prayer in the Dome of the Prophet, asking God not to let him die when she was still a child, he realized how much he feared that she might meet the same fate he had. He feared that she might find herself an orphan, alone.

His mother had died two weeks after he was born from child-birth fever, and his father had followed her a year later.

For a long time he had asked God not to let him die when Leen was still a child. The thought of it terrified him before she was born, and it terrified him even more after she was born. His father's paternal cousin had supported him when he was a boy. But who would support Leen? Her grandfather was an elderly man, and her maternal cousin was a teenager who was still wet behind the ears and hadn't seen life's troubles yet. And she didn't have an older brother. She would go to ruin in no time. If he, a man, had gone to ruin, how would she avoid the same fate if he left her young and alone? Something inside him had been damaged. He was aware of his weakness and his terrible aloneness, and he'd discovered how debilitating it is to be born, then be left to face this life on one's own.

When he'd seen Malek two days earlier, he'd realized what a tremendous burden it is to be the father of a girl like Leen. However, he'd had no choice but to say to him what he'd said that evening: 'Forgive me, son, but I can't just cast my daughter aside and let people destroy her.'

'But sir, are you saying that if you let her marry me you'll be casting her aside?'

'Not at all, son. But you're enlightened and perceptive, and you know what I mean. The problem isn't with you. It's with the people who have no compassion. And I can't expose my daughter to that kind of treatment.'

'And what concern are other people to us? You can stop them in their tracks. This is your daughter, sir, and her happiness is more important to you than other people. Or am I wrong?'

'Of course it is, son. But . . .'

'But what, sir? You've given me your answer without even thinking. And without consulting your daughter!'

'No offense, son, but it's simply out of the question. I've told you that I can't let my daughter be treated that way.'

'Is it because I'm black, sir?'

The question remained suspended in the void between them as he thought about how to extricate himself from the snare in which it had landed him. If he said no, he would be lying, and if he said yes, he would hurt Malek. But he was, in fact, black. And if *he* didn't look at his color, other people would look at nothing *but* his color. They would harass and ostracize Leen, and she wouldn't be able to bear it because they would never stop. Every time they saw the two of them together they would get that hateful, disapproving look on their faces, since a lot of people in his country, when they saw a black man and a white woman walking together, wouldn't think they were husband and wife. Suspicions and questions would haunt them wherever they went. He wanted to tell Malek this, but he couldn't find the words he needed to say it without hurting a man he was meeting for the first time.

'Don't send me away disappointed, sir.'

'God is the one who brings happiness, and there's bound to be a girl that's right for you somewhere out there.'

He didn't know how the phrase had slipped out, but it had. Malek smiled forlornly, saying, 'I'm not going to consider this a final answer. Take your time, sir, and think about it. And I'll be in touch with you again.'

The father's smile, puny and wan, seemed to contain a glimmer of approval. But as Malek turned to leave, he caught a glimpse of the bruises that covered him, and at that moment he wished he hadn't lived to see that day. He'd already known that life was ugly. But he'd never thought it could be both ugly and depraved.

He wondered if he was rejecting Malek because he was black, or because other people would reject him. For a moment he suspected that he was being pulled into the mire along with the others, and that all he had looked at was color. But how could he do otherwise?

Oh God.

Up to that point in his life he'd never had to put his convictions about people's color or race on the line. But now he was faced with an onerous test, and whether he passed it or failed it, it would be excruciating. He remembered sitting in gatherings where someone would tell the story of so-and-so's daughter who was engaged to be married to a half-breed, a Barnawi, or to somebody from the Falata tribe, the Hausa tribe, or whatever. He would listen quietly to the other men's comments and complaints, then say without a moment's hesitation, 'Listen, everybody. It's a matter of destiny, that's all. If her family approves, that's it. Nobody has any right to interfere. You can't judge people by their color.'

Ha-a-a-a-a-a-a-a-a-a-a-a-a-a!

He laughed bitterly as he heard himself spouting platitudes, the ones you read in books and hear on soap operas, and as he slaughtered his daughter with the frightening reality that she thought she could face alone.

'You can't judge people by their color.'

No, no, no, no. No matter how many times a person might say it, it still didn't make it true, because people here *did* judge others by their color, their tribe, their race and their ethnic origin. And he was no exception to the rule. He hadn't succeeded in being that exception. Leen thought people would raise a ruckus for a while, then get distracted with their own lives. But she was wrong. She would remain under their watchful eye forever. She would be sickened by their curiosity and their occasionally dirty, revolting insinuations. And she would be even more sickened when she saw the way they treated her children.

If he said yes, things would spin out of his control, and his daughter would be lost. He had prayed to God not to afflict him through her, and now he was about to lose her once and for all. But no, he couldn't lose her now. Not now. Not now. Not now.

7

What's under the color

As virtual war broke out in Qatar in preparation for a US military strike against Iraq, US forces in Kuwait completed their preparations to take part in any conflict that might erupt in the region. According to Colonel Kenneth Gantt, Commander of the 9th Field Artillery Regiment ('Battlekings'), his forces in Kuwait 'are expecting a telephone call from US President George Bush commanding us to move to topple Saddam Hussein'. In a press statement following maneuvers that took place yesterday in northern Kuwait, Gantt added, 'We are ready to use force at any time, and we are fully prepared to do so.'

Dubar ✶ *the 7th of Wail,*
the twelfth year after Desert Storm

Hajjaj ibnYusuf asked for the hand of 'Abdullah ibn Ja'far's daughter, Umm Kulthum, for a dowry of 2 million dirhems in secret, and 500,000 dirhems in public. 'Abdullah ibn Ja'far agreed to the marriage, and Hajjaj took Umm Kulthum to Iraq, where she lived with him for eight months. When 'Abdullah ibn Ja'far went out as an emissary to the Umayyad Caliph 'Abd al-Malik ibn Marwan, he stayed in Damascus. While there, he received a visit from al-Walid, 'Abd al-Malik's son, who came to him mounted on a mule accompanied by a group of men. 'Abdullah ibn Ja'far welcomed them warmly.

'But I do not welcome *you*!' retorted al-Walid.

'Wait a moment, nephew,' 'Abdullah ibn Ja'far replied. 'I do not deserve for you to say such a thing to me!'

'Oh, yes, you do,' retorted al-Walid, 'and even worse!'

'And why is that?'

Al-Walid replied, 'Because you took the best of the Arabs' womenfolk, the highest-ranking of the women of 'Abd Manaf, and gave her in marriage to a lowly servant of the Thaqif tribe.'

'And for this you find fault with me, nephew?'

'Yes, I do.'

'I swear to God,' 'Abdullah replied, 'no one has less right to blame me for this than you and your father do.

119

The governors who preceded you took care to preserve family ties, and they recognized my rights. As for you and your father, you refused to provide me with financial support until I found myself ridden with debt. I swear to God, if a pug-nosed Ethiopian slave gave me what this "lowly servant of Thaqif" has given me, I would give my daughter to him in marriage, and I would use the dowry money to pay off my debts.'

Saying no more to him, al-Walid turned his mount and departed. He then went to see 'Abd al-Malik.

'What troubles you, Abu 'Abbas?' 'Abd al-Malik asked.

'You have given so much power and authority to this lowly servant of Thaqif that he has taken the women of Banu 'Abd Manaf in marriage.'

Seized suddenly with tribal fervor, 'Abd al-Malik wrote a letter to Hajjaj telling him that no sooner had he set his letter down than he was to divorce Umm Kulthum. So he divorced her. However, Hajjaj never ceased to provide her with material support, and he continued to treat her with dignity until she passed out of this world. He also maintained his ties with 'Abdullah ibn Ja'far until his death. Not a year passed but that Hajjaj sent him a caravan laden with money, clothing and rarities. (Ahmad al-Abshihi, *al-Mustatraf fi Kulli Fann Mustazraf*)

Her father said, 'I can't put my daughter in harm's way.'

Malek couldn't go on arguing with him for long. How could he when Leen's father had given voice to the very thing that had kept going through his own mind ever since he met her? He'd even spoken to her once about it. Maybe he hadn't said it in exactly the same words. However, he had said it, and she had heard it. He didn't believe she had thought of it in the way he had. On the other hand, maybe she had, but had assumed – stubborn woman that she was – that she was up to the confrontation.

He remembered how, at the time he'd said it, she'd been sitting across from him with a smile on her face. He'd resisted an urge to place his fingers along the base of her neck, over her right collarbone. He'd continued to observe her breathing, mesmerized by the way her delicate skin went up and down so evenly. He was gripped momentarily by a certainty – a certainty that later became constant – that she had been made for him to love her. He hadn't thought about where this certainty had come from or how it had come. However, he knew that if he had met her in another place, he would still have loved her, that if he had met her in another time, he would still have loved her, and that . . . if his skin were a different color, he would still have loved her. When he took a careful look at his certainty – with her sitting tranquilly across from him as though life had yet to touch her with pain – he smiled, since he realized how fragile this certainty was, and how easily it could be destroyed, how very easily it could be destroyed. Even so, it flowed through his deepest parts as though he'd been made to embrace it.

'Why are you smiling?' she asked him.

He said, 'I was thinking about how, even if my skin were a different color, I would still have loved you.'

She knit her brow slightly, then asked, 'Why is it that when you look at us, all you see is the color?'

'I see what you don't see, Leen.'

He blew the smoke from his cigarette far away before saying, 'I don't know exactly what it is that makes you so different. But you've swum far away from life's filth, and when I met you and got close to you, I smelled the fragrance of your heart. Your heart smells like apples. That's why I've held onto you. I didn't want my heart to turn into some fetid swamp. I was being carried away toward a life of filth since I thought I didn't have anything left to lose, and that I should hurt others the way I'd been hurt. But then you came along, and now I should keep you from getting hurt. That's why I see the color.'

'Nobody has the power to spare others harm. I'm bound to suffer my share of it no matter how much it happens to be.'

'But I mustn't be a cause of harm to you.'

'If you really don't want to harm me, then you mustn't die.'

Falling silent for a moment, he buried his cigarette butt in an ashtray in front of him. Then he said, 'All right, then. *You* die.'

With a mournful smile she said, 'So my dying wouldn't hurt you! Al-l-l-l right. Tomorrow I'll die, though I hate ordinary death.'

She laughed, and so did he.

He wished he could call her on the phone right then and say, 'Why don't you die now?' And she would say, 'OK, I'll die, even though I don't like ordinary death.'

Then he would laugh even if she didn't. He would look for his cheap cigarette lighter so that he could light a cigarette that he would put out before he'd smoked even half of it, since he'd lost hope, and it was impossible to find any solace.

For as long as he'd known her he'd tried not to get carried away with his dreams, since he reckoned he knew more about life here than she did, and that he should be careful not to let hope do them in. Curses on hope. So, after her father had tactfully turned him down the evening before, he understood what she meant when she said, 'I'm not going to torture myself with hope twice.'

Once he'd become aware of his situation, he'd stopped dreaming altogether, since at some point he'd realized that his dreams, however small they might be, were too big for someone with knotty circumstances like his. It had taken him a long time to comprehend the fact that his father hadn't committed some sin by not attempting to obtain an 'absolution', and that his own failure and disappointment had nothing to do with what his father had been thinking when he arrived more than fifty years earlier. He'd emigrated from his country to . . . God, his dream to be near the Sacred Mosque in Mecca. He hadn't left his homeland for the sake of an 'absolution'.

This has been God's land ever since the creation of Adam. So who would drive God's creatures out of God's land?

Had this been his father's logic? He didn't know, and sometimes he hoped never to know. All he knew, and all he experienced time and time again, was that when it came to proving someone's identity, people didn't think about God, God's creatures, or God's land. All they thought about was official papers: the little magnetized card, the disgusting rectangular 'family book', and the passport with its green cover displaying two swords uprooting a palm tree in shiny gold. And every time the question revolved around identity, he had none of these documents in his pocket. He was so marginal that when a traffic policeman checked his identification at a traffic light, he even disapproved of his wearing traditional Saudi garb. After looking at his license, he would

123

say, 'Well, well, well! You've even got yourself looking just like one of us! Let me see your residence card.'

And to the extent that he was marginal, he was lost. For more than thirty years the only homeland he'd known was this sand that stretched from the Arabian Gulf to the Red Sea. Yet still, there was no room for him there.

11:30 p.m.

> It has been said that Ham lay with his wife on the ark and that, in response, Noah cursed him, praying for his offspring to be disfigured. Consequently, a black son was born to him. This son was Canaan son of Ham, forefather of the Sudanese people. Alternatively, it has been said that Ham saw his father sleeping with his private parts exposed, but failed to conceal them. Seeing the state of their father, his brothers then covered him up. Consequently, Noah prayed that Ham's sperm would mutate and that his offspring would be slaves to his brothers. (Ibn Kathir, *al-Bidayah wal-Nihayah*)

He spread his hands in front of his face, then began turning them over and examining them. He remembered how Leen had once rubbed the back of his hand with her forefinger, saying, 'I want to see what's under the color.'

The color! How far away color had taken him, though he hadn't realized – as he moved away – how brutish he'd become before he met her. Then he looked at life through her and saw the ruinous end he would have met if their paths hadn't crossed.

He didn't often talk to her about color. Would she understand if he told her that he'd suffered so much that he'd stopped looking at his color and hurting, and that after she came along, he'd begun looking at it and feeling pain all over again? And if she did understand, wouldn't she be pained herself?

His mother would tell him from time to time that he was the most handsome of her sons, and the one that looked most like her father. He believed the part about looking like her father. But he couldn't believe that anything black could be nice to look at, and when Leen said to him, 'You're handsome,' he laughed and said sarcastically, 'But not more handsome than Majed Abdullah!'

She didn't reply. Later she admitted that she regretted having told him how charmed she was by his looks. He responded the way he responded to others. He contented himself with a little smile of resignation as he listened to her, since she didn't know what he'd been through on account of color. She hadn't been with him on the day his friends raised a ruckus because he objected to their insistence that a certain actress was beautiful on account of her color:

'Hey, man, it's enough that she's white!'

'Damn, is she good-lookin'!'

He looked over at his four friends. All of them were black. He felt uncertainty pricking him like a hot pinhead. One hesitant voice against four convinced black voices, all of which were saying that whiteness equals beauty. Whiteness alone. Whiteness, even if it covers lackluster features or a malicious spirit, since whiteness would atone for all a person's faults.

Iqbal, the Pakistani man who worked at the corner store near their house, was in the habit of greeting him cheerfully as 'Blackie'. He would say it so unthinkingly, Malek didn't feel as though he could get angry with him, or with the name. He had no choice but to disregard its sharp blade: the sharp blade of having color as his identity, the card by means of which people recognized him and which defined him for them. In his life, color had become a painful blow that he would never know how to return, not because he was weak or powerless, but, rather, because the other color had never been an insult or a dirty name. The inferiority of his color was as old as the hills, so old that he was in no position, now, to deny it even if he barricaded himself behind a thousand sayings of the Prophet or verses from the Qur'an. Consequently, he'd stopped hurting. He'd stopped viewing the issue as his own personal war. He'd even stopped getting upset when some angry driver hurled vulgar epithets at him through his car window for not moving faster when the traffic light turned yellow. 'God damn you, kur!' or, 'Shame on whoever let you have a car, you slave!'

None of these labels – *kur, takruni, kuwayha* – hurt the way they had in long years past, when the lofty idea of justice still burned brightly deep inside him. In the beginning he'd never thought, even for a moment, that this ideal would disintegrate inside him along with his certainty that it could be realized. As it was, he'd lost his certainty of lots of things he'd once thought he was meant to experience and achieve.

Justice!

What a ridiculous idea!

He'd suffered no end on account of this idea. However, his pain had led him to another idea that had relieved him some-what and protected him from going downhill more badly than he already had. This new idea was that God is just even though life is unjust for the most part. If justice were achieved in life, there would have been nothing to explain Satan's overween-ing pride, the creation of Heaven and Hell, or all the pain, anguish and despair people endure. He'd clung to this little faith to the best of his ability so that he wouldn't stop believing in God's justice, which he'd been on the verge of doing.

He'd been thirteen years old when the pain associated with his color first crushed him, and its impact had confused him for long years thereafter. At the time he hadn't understood why it was happening to him:

'How far do you think you'll get?'

The question was posed to Malek one day by the middle school's assistant principal after he'd called him to his office. He hadn't understood the question. Besides, he had been so flustered, he hadn't known whether the man was asking him the question in order for him to answer it, or as a rebuke. He hadn't known until the man went on, saying, 'They say your grades are high. So I'm wondering why you're going to all this trouble. I mean, you know as well as I do that if you get the chance to finish high school, you still won't get a chance to graduate from university. So why put yourself through all this? Give the chance to somebody else in this country. At the very least, return the favor to the country that took you and your family in. Otherwise, you'd be hanging around parking lots with a pail and washrag waiting for a signal from some-body to wash his car.'

He hadn't known what to do or say. He hadn't even known what to feel when he heard those words. The room kept getting smaller and smaller and smaller as he stood there, star-ing at some nebulous point in front of him.

Then finally the man had said to him, 'Go back to your class.'

As he walked down the corridors, he could hear the sound of his ribs shattering like sheets of glass under the colossal pressure of the pain. He couldn't tell anyone what had happened to him. By the end of the week he'd moved to another seat in the class because he couldn't bear to look the assistant principal's son Abdulaziz – who sat next to him and who, irony of ironies, was his friend – in the face. Every time their eyes met, he saw the words he had heard his friend's father say leaping about like tiny flaming masses with scornful, demonic features. He didn't want to hurt Abdulaziz because he wasn't bad. At least, he hadn't been during the two years he'd known him. They'd played and laughed together, concluded make-believe alliances, hatched little plots, and been harassed by their other friends. But there was no way it could go on any longer.

He opened up a deep pit inside himself and began throwing everything into it. He didn't even wait to hear the sound of all those details crashing against the bottom of his sorrow and anguish. Then he moved away from the pit, the things inside it, Abdulaziz, and even himself. He no longer concerned himself with striving for what he wanted, since he'd concluded that he wanted things, but they didn't want him, or that he wasn't worthy to want anything. He was too young to bear the pain alone. But he couldn't get anyone to share it with him, so he buried it and went on, the way children tend to do when pain is too great for them to endure.

He began giving up his dreams one after another. He started by not getting high grades anymore. Then he stopped being torn between studying medicine and studying engineering, since he'd thrown the pursuit of either of these goals into the pit he'd opened inside himself for all his hopes and aspirations.

Never in his life had he met a black doctor. So what was the point of wondering whether he should study medicine or engineering?

He did his best to get into high school, although he no longer aspired to anything beyond finishing high school, then getting a job – any job – that would enable him to make enough money to leave this country once and for all. For years, bitterness had been building up inside him like salt stalactites in a deep, lightless cave, and over the years, everything over which his bitterness had accumulated had fallen to pieces. And together with the bitterness there was fear. He was terribly afraid, not wanting to meet the kind of fate that had met others of his race who faced situations like his: Ibrahim, whose brain had been damaged from sniffing glue; Ahmad, who'd been driven by provocative words to murder another young man in an altercation that had broken out between them; Hussein, who'd disappeared, after which they heard he'd been killed by anti-drug police . . . And the list went on. These were people who had been born to find that life's fabric had been cut out for them in such a way that they had no choice but to squeeze themselves into it and go on, grateful and content, in the narrow margin left to them. And as they went, they had to be careful not to leave the margin for life's mainstream, since otherwise, there were more people than they might think standing ready to give them a kick in the seat of the pants. It was unacceptable for a black to distinguish himself to the point where others were obliged to remain grudgingly silent as they watched him leave his narrow margin to join them on life's broad highways and byways.

The dark fates he so feared weren't restricted to members of his own race. However, they were more noticeable among them than they were among others. It was as though such fates attracted people of his race with an irresistible magnetic force, and he was afraid that some day he might find himself within their field, unarmed with anything but his anguish and despair.

Munis ★ *the 8th of Wail,*
the twelfth year after Desert Storm
1 a.m.

. . . Bilal, a slave to the Banu Jumah tribe among whom he
had been born and raised, was later emancipated by Abu
Bakr, may God be pleased with him. His full name was
Bilal ibn Rabah and his mother's name was Hamamah. He
was sincere in his Islamic faith and pure of heart. His
master, Umayyah ibn Wahb ibn Hudhayfah ibn Jumah,
used to take him out in the midday heat to Mecca's open
country. He would issue instructions for a huge, heavy
stone to be placed on Bilal's chest. Then he would say to
him, 'You will stay this way until you die, or until you
renounce your faith in Muhammad and worship the gods
al-Lat and al-'Uzza.' In response Bilal would simply repeat,
'One, One . . .' (Ibn Hisham, *The Life of Muhammad*)

'One, One, One, One . . .'
Many years earlier Malek had heard an actor repeat this
phrase on the television screen, and for several evenings he'd
watched the man being tortured without saying anything but,
'One, One . . .' Throughout that entire time he kept thinking
about one thing: that the actor was a white man who'd been
painted black. He'd noticed it from the way the color was
distributed around the man's lips, eyes and palms, and most of
all, from the actor's features, which bore no resemblance to

those of any black man. Over time, and after seeing lots of white men painted black on the screen, he began to think that black people were so torpid, they weren't fit to play the roles of black men or tell their stories, and that if he wanted his story to be told the way it ought to be, he would have to sit in front of a TV screen and see it done by white people who'd painted themselves black. In any case, the number of black people whose stories were worth telling was hardly worth mentioning. So why think this way?

He would try to think back to the time when he first became aware of the difference in his color, but he couldn't. He remembered the first time he'd been violently crushed on account of his color and his situation. However, he couldn't recall when he'd first looked at his color and seen it.

When he was in high school, he'd been sitting alone in the schoolyard one day when a classmate of his by the name of Husam came and sat down beside him. After running the tip of a pen through the sand in front of them for a moment, Husam said, 'I'd like to ask you a question, but I'm afraid you'll get mad.'

'Go ahead.'

A heavy silence descended. Then Husam said hesitantly, 'When a person's black, how does he feel?'

Malek looked into his classmate's face and, seeing no cruelty, restrained the impulse to blurt out an angry retort. He bowed his head as he thought about the question. He couldn't help but notice the unspoken assumption that lay behind the question; namely, that black people are so different that they almost seem beyond the pale of humanity. They're so different, they don't feel in the same way people do, and maybe they don't hurt, either.

He let out a slow breath. Then, without looking at Husam, he said, 'Would you like to trade places?'

'You want to know the truth, and you won't get mad?'

'Of course.'

'Actually, I wouldn't. When people call me Baqaya Hujjaj or Tarsh Bahr, it makes me really mad. So how would I feel if I were Tarsh Bahr and black, too!?'

His words were followed by an even heavier, more oner- ous silence, which was broken by Husam, who said, 'I hope you're not mad!'

Smiling, Malek looked his classmate in the face and said, 'Why should I be? I'm a nigger, you're some trash that washed up from the sea, and some other guys are "Serbian Bedouins". Everybody gets what's coming to him from everybody else, and nobody's better than anybody else.'

Husam laughed, but Malek couldn't share in his laugh- ter. He didn't see anything funny about it. All he saw was something agonizingly painful that he couldn't under- stand, just the way he couldn't understand how the books he studied could tell the story of Bilal ibn Rabah with such reverence while, most of the time, his color and origins were treated with contempt. Accounts like these seemed so remote from what he experienced every day, he'd suspected for some time that he must be reading legends somebody had thought up out of his head. Nor had he found any evidence to convince him otherwise. He hadn't found a single branch to cling to lest he fall headlong into the sea of racism in which life around him was floating: Bedouins – city folks; Hejazi – Nejdi – Qubayli – Khudhayri; artisan – businessman; 110 – 220; slave – *kur* – *kuwayha* – *tarsh bahr* – *baqaya hujjaj*.

Even his mother said to him, 'Watch out for Arab girls, son.'

He'd never argued with her. It had never even occurred to him to argue with her. As he heard her say the words, he would observe a faint smile playing at the corners of her lips. It was a collusive smile that expressed her delight in his manhood more than a genuine attitude toward Arab girls. Consequently, he hadn't felt any need to justify to himself the fact that he listened to her without questioning what she said. After all, life around him was going the way it was going, and if he stopped for a moment to modify its course, it would just trample him underfoot and go on. After all, he wasn't a prophet or a wealthy man. He was a black alien.

1:15 a.m.
> I loved her by chance despite the enmity between her
> people and mine
> And never, by your father's life, can my desire be fulfilled.
>   ('Antarah ibn Shaddad)

The first time he asked her if they could meet, he'd expected her to refuse. However, she surprised him by agreeing to it. It had been seven months since their first telephone conversation, during which time he'd been swept off his feet so thoroughly that he was ready to take a risk. He couldn't contain his infatuation with her voice, which had a deep, calm ring to it. But what charmed him most of all was the way she said 'Allô'.

Once he said to her, 'You sound as though you're of French extraction.'

A long 'N-o-o-o-o, you!' escaped her lips. Then she laughed.

'No, really!' he said. 'You say "Allô" with an exquisite French accent!'

As on all the other occasions when he'd complimented her on her voice, her laugh, or her way of thinking, she made no comment. He assumed her silence was simply a way of not hurting his feelings. He thought maybe she was counting on him to realize all the barriers that stood between them, and that she didn't want to be the one to cut him off.

Even so, he found himself being inexorably drawn to her. He threw caution to the wind, along with his silence and his unending desire for life to go away and for his present to be transformed into a past that he could leave behind and never look back at again. To his surprise he suddenly noticed that life had begun awakening inside him, and that he'd begun to change. As he realized this he felt afraid, because he had deep feelings for her, but didn't know what lay hidden around the next bend.

He'd changed so much that, after having laughed at the love stories in songs, soap operas and movies, he caught himself picturing her on his pillow or repeating her name, feeling for a fleeting moment that his mind was devoid of everything. It seemed as though her name was being repeated like the murmur of a pearly ornament suspended from the ceiling of his room. If a puff of air touched it, it would tinkle with a mysterious faintness that resurrected vague memories from their resting places. Her name resurrected memories that had been hiding in places that, until that moment, he couldn't have identified. One of them seemed like a memory of him fleeing from someone down an unidentified street, laughing and soaking wet. Another showed him standing at the door to their house wearing new clothes while his mother flitted about the house, spraying rosewater out of a spray can. In another he was sitting in a room, very little of whose furniture he could recall, as his mother handed him a plate of Labaniya, saying, 'Happy New Year, son.'

He wanted to tell Leen about all these images, and others too. He wanted badly to let her see what he saw every night when, enclosed within the walls of his room, the details of his day would leave him and all that would remain was her voice, her words, and her laugh. This was why he'd asked her if they could meet. He'd prepared himself for the worst, since he hadn't expected anything but either a sharp no or a subtle rebuff. But instead, she'd shattered all his expectations. In fact, ever since he'd met her she'd been shattering his negative expectations.

'All right,' she'd said. 'Why not?'

And now, in the darkness of the night and the sorrow that enveloped his soul, he closed his eyes and remembered how awkward he'd felt when she sat down across from him and he saw her face for the first time. He'd sat back in his chair slightly so as to give himself more distance across which to contemplate her. The strangest thing he'd realized when he saw her beauty was that he'd been counting on her not being beautiful. In fact, he'd hoped she wouldn't be beautiful! As soon as he realized this, he knew that desolation had eaten away at him so deeply that he'd become small in his own eyes, afraid of having to pay the price for receiving what he really deserved. However, at that time he hadn't wanted to think about desolation. He was so anxious, he had wanted to say what was on his mind, all at once and without stopping. True, the coffee shop hadn't been crowded. He had chosen a rather secluded corner, and had asked the waiter to surround their table with room dividers that would insulate them from the world around them. Even so, anxiety had been tearing him to pieces, since curiosity was the order of the day, and their contrasting colors were certain to arouse both curiosity and suspicion. So how would he be able to protect her from others' crudity if he couldn't even protect himself?

Later, when it became possible for them to meet far from others' inquisitive gazes, he told her that her beauty had rather taken him by surprise. It wasn't a dazzling sort of beauty. Nor, however, was it an ordinary beauty or the kind of beauty one could easily forget. When, long after their first meeting, he passed the tip of his forefinger over her lower lip, he thought he would never recover from it, and that he would go on thinking about her even if he went into a coma some day.

1:20 a.m.

When night had fallen Yahya heard the screams of the women whose men had been slain. He asked what it was he was hearing, and when someone told him, he said, 'After daybreak kill the women and the children.' They did so, and the killing went on for three days. In his camp there was a commander with three thousand black soldiers who took the women by force. By the third day Yahya had finished slaying the people of Mosul, and on the fourth day he rode out with spears and drawn swords. As he departed he was waylaid by a woman who took hold of his mount's reins. His companions wanted to kill her, but he forbade them. She said to him, 'Are you not from the tribe of Bani Hesham? Are you not a paternal cousin of the Messenger of God, may God's blessings and peace be upon him? Do you not deem it beneath the dignity of Muslim

137

Arab women to be raped by black men?' Making no reply, but moved by her words, Yahya had one of his men escort her to a safe place. (Ibn al-Athir, *al-Kamil fil-Tarikh*)

From the time he realized he was falling for her, he'd made a point of letting her know what color he was. His intense concern about the matter made him realize that he viewed his color as a handicap that he felt obliged to inform her of before she discovered it for herself. But, although he spoke to her about his color, he postponed telling her about the matter of the 'absolution'. He'd thought he would tell her about it later, but he never had, not because he hadn't wanted to, but because he hadn't known where the path would lead them.

By the time he met her, he'd despaired even of his despair. He'd been living his life without expecting to get anywhere. He went on because he had to go on. Four years after finishing high school he'd decided to postpone the idea of emigrating indefinitely. After all, how could he emigrate when the salary he collected at the end of every month seemed like so much salt that dissolved in the sweat on his palms: a few grains that he clutched tightly in his fist only to find that when he unclenched it, he had barely enough to meet his personal needs and those of his mother and his brother. His father had died long before. He'd died so long before, in fact, that he'd forgotten many of his features. His maternal uncle had supported them for years, but as soon as Malek got a job, the situation had changed, and he'd become the household's sole breadwinner.

He'd moved from job to job, institution to institution and company to company before settling at the archives of a private clinic. More than three years earlier he'd run into a friend from high school. In the course of their conversation he'd learned that his friend was working as a freelance reporter for a local newspaper. His friend had suggested that he try his luck at the same newspaper, because they needed someone to provide them with news items, coverage, reports, interviews, and it was this happenstance that had led him to Leen.

There were moments when he'd wished that happenstance had never occurred. He'd been dejected. Love had been eating away at him without his seeing even the faintest glimmer of light. He wondered what sort of a crime it was for him to love her and want to marry her. What was it that would make it impossible for him to do so? His color? Why did people make his color into a sin that nothing could wash away? When they did this they seemed to be saying to God, 'You created a color that's bad!' But why was he wondering about such things when he was almost certain that there was nothing that could heal the sickness in his soul? No one – not even Leen – could feel and understand what had happened to him at the moment when he realized that he was bound inextricably to an outcast's color that he hadn't chosen for himself, to a situation he'd done nothing to create, and to a country in whose vast fabric he'd wanted so desperately to be a tiny thread.

He wished he could let out a long scream. For as long as he'd known her he'd been hearing the scream of the being deep inside him. It was a frightful scream that neither fell silent nor brought relief. For as long as he'd known her he'd felt cheated, and that his life – his entire life – wasn't his. He'd lived it, but it hadn't been his. He'd had another life, but it had been wrested away from him. Or, rather, he'd allowed it to be wrested from him. Only much later did he realize that he'd relinquished his own rights, and Leen's rights too. Meanwhile, in his heart of hearts, he believed he was less than what she deserved. He hadn't completed his education, he didn't have an 'absolution', and he hadn't been fierce enough not to give in without a fight. He'd realized too late that he'd been led away to the fate that others wanted for him, and that the fates he'd fled from were no worse than his present capitulation. As for the people around him, they would think he was unworthy of Leen for the simple reason that he was black. In their eyes she would be too good for him – so much so that they would give themselves the right to condemn, and to nastily wonder aloud what would make her want to be associated with him. They would even go so far as to refuse to marry their daughters to her brother or to allow her sisters to marry (if she had had sisters) because, like leprosy, his color was something that could only be coped with by avoidance.

A year after meeting her, and after realizing that she'd found a place in his heart, he'd begun applying for an 'absolution'. All the papers he could get his hands on that might demonstrate his right to citizenship – his birth certificate, his diplomas, a certificate of good conduct from the local chief of police, a tattered document testifying to the fact that his mother had been born in the country – he gathered together and organized into a green file. Then he started getting his hopes up, and decided not to mention it to her in the hope that he would be able to tell her the story some day. 'Imagine!' he'd say. 'When I first met you I still didn't have an "absolution"!' Then he would laugh, and she would open her black eyes wide as saucers, saying, 'You're kidding!'

But he hadn't said, 'Imagine . . .!', and she hadn't replied, 'You're kidding!' The whole thing had turned into numbers, dates and little pieces of paper with appointments written on them that he would stuff into the breast pocket of his robe. He would take the little pieces of paper with him to Riyadh only to come back home with still more of them, but without being told by anyone at the Ministry of the Interior whether he should get his hopes up or stop hoping altogether. One day he'd asked a ministry employee, 'Can you tell me if there's any hope?'

The employee had looked at him for several moments before saying in a serious tone, 'Have you got really good connections? Or can you play soccer?'

He shook his head sadly, and the employee said nothing more. Even the sound of the papers the employee was shuffling died. There then came the moment when he realized that putting off the announcement of unpleasant news only makes it all the more unpleasant. The matter of the 'absolution' had turned into a sharp bend in the road. As they rounded it, he and Leen were about to go careening into a dark wasteland, and he couldn't blame her for a thing.

It had been a long year since he'd applied for the 'absolution' and two years since they'd met, when she asked him impassively, 'Haven't we been in love for a long time now?'

He understood what she meant, and he loved her dearly for having said what she said in that particular way and tone. He heaved a deep sigh, inwardly cursing everything and everyone that stood between them. Then he said, 'Listen, Leen. I've got a bit of a dilemma on my hands that has nothing to do with you and doesn't concern you. I'm trying to resolve it, and once I've done that, the road ahead will open up for us.'

'It has nothing to do with me and doesn't concern me? Does that mean I don't have a right to know what it is?'

'Let's not go there, all right? But I swear to you that I'll tell you about it as soon as I've resolved it.'

'When will that be?'

The question tore into his heart, hot and merciless. He resisted the pain as he said to her, 'I really don't know. But let's hope it will be soon.'

She had asked him about the dilemma a number of times after that. She'd asked him laughingly, worriedly, furiously. Then there came the time when she said to him, 'Not understanding hurts. I've tried to understand why you're stalling, but I've failed, and I can't take it anymore. I can't go on being in the shadow of your life in this land of suspicion. Three years have gone by, and that's too much. It's longer than I'd expected, and it's longer than I can take. It's also longer than I can forgive myself for if I sit down some day and think about the story with my mind. And you know my mind.'

There descended a gray silence, heavy as lead. Then, with some effort, he said, 'You're right.'

'So then, if you'll excuse me . . .' She hung up without giving him the chance to say a thing. And what could he have said to stop the steeds of suspicion that had gone galloping through her deepest places? What word could have taken her back to before the moment when she said, '. . . you're stalling'? Or to the moment when, after an intimate meeting, she'd written to him saying:

'I wanted to see what your touch might do to the woman hidden deep inside me, the woman who'd slept for so many years that I'd begun to think nothing and nobody could wake her up. Seeing her asleep peacefully there in the darkness, I thought I might have lost my mind so completely that I'd fled for all those years from letting a man touch me intimately. But actually, the issue isn't whether you touch me, but, rather, whether I love you so much that I wait passionately for you to touch me.'

He'd smoked a lot of cigarettes that night, drunk cup after cup of coffee and tea, and read her few letters. Then he'd gone over the text messages from her that were saved on his cell phone. For a moment he was suffocated by his sense of impotence. He hated the 'absolution' and the raunchy taste of coffee when someone gulps it down cold after a long drag on a cigarette. And even more than that, he hated the cold voice that kept repeating mechanically whenever he called her, 'The mobile number you are dialing is currently unavailable. Please try later.'

Afraid of losing her, he was gripped suddenly by a desperate desire to erase the world. It was the same desire that had come over him for the first time years before as he ran through the hospital lobby in search of someone to help him carry his brother Yusuf, who lay spattered with blood in the car at the hospital gate.

He'd gotten home late that night. Then, as usual, he'd gone to see his brother in his room. But no sooner had he opened the door than he saw the blood, which was forming a small, dark, viscous pool on the covers where Yusuf lay.

'Yusuf!' he screamed in terror.

He didn't think of calling an ambulance. He didn't even wait to figure out what had caused his only brother to cut his own artery. He didn't wait to figure it out because he himself had come to the same precipice from which Yusuf had flung himself. Unlike Yusuf, however, he hadn't been able to close his eyes and descend into the lightless abyss of despair. Instead he had retreated at the last moment, perhaps in order to grab his brother and bring him back. He still didn't know how he'd picked Yusuf up and run with him to the car, or how he'd driven to the Dharbat al-Shams Hospital without seeing anyone or anything the entire way. He hadn't been the least bit self-conscious when, in search of help, he ran through the emergency-unit entrance, his robe spattered with blood.

When help did come, he stood at a distance watching two orderlies transfer his brother from the car to a stretcher, then rush him to the emergency room. Meanwhile, he began thinking about his mother, who had been left alone sleeping in the house, and how she would panic if she woke up and didn't find the two of them.

'O God, don't let her panic,' he prayed, 'and bring Yusuf back to her.'

He'd seen Yusuf's desperation. However, he hadn't seen the depth of his despondency. One night he'd heard him blow up in his mother's face when she scolded him for coming home late.

'So do you want me to sit around at home like a woman?!'

'No. But don't be late and make me worry about you. And if you do have to be late, call.'

'Like, what's going to happen to me?'

'Son . . .'

Interrupting her irritably, he said, 'Why did you have me, anyway? So that I could live in torment?'

'Have some fear of God, Yusuf. What's the matter with you?'

'I'm fed up! I mean, do you like the way my life is, Mom? I can't even get a middle-school diploma since I don't have any connections to get me into the school, and there's no work.'

'Things will be better tomorrow.'

'God damn tomorrow.'

'Shame on you! What do you lack?'

'What I lack is to be a human being in other people's eyes.'

'God forbid! What are you, then? An animal?'

But Yusuf made no reply. Instead, he stomped off to his room and slammed the door behind him. His mother's murmurs grew louder and louder, but it didn't occur to Malek to go out and check on them, since anguish had taken him to the same barren island from whose edges Yusuf was shrieking, and he thought Yusuf would know how to survive, since he was shrieking in rejection of everything he encountered, whereas he, Malek, had succumbed to silence and abysses, filling them with his days and pieces of his life, then moving on without looking back. Not for a moment had he thought that Yusuf was shrieking because he was frightened and unable to survive – not, that is, until he saw the pool of blood under him.

He looked over at his brother lying there with a stillness that shot him through with sorrow. He thought about how he was going to tell his mother what had happened. Bad news is exhausting, and sometimes it seems easier to receive it than it is to announce it. Yet soon he found himself announcing it.

She turned to him with a bewildered look on her face. Then, in a tone that killed him, she asked, 'Are you talking to me about *my* Yusuf?'

He nodded.

'Your brother Yusuf slit his own throat?'

'He tried to, Mom, but we got to him in time.'

She looked at him for a moment, then got up and headed for her room. Before going in, she turned to him and said, 'Your brother died a long time ago. The person in the hospital isn't my son.'

'Mom . . .'

But she just went into her room and closed the door. After that she refused to visit Yusuf in the hospital. She refused even to say that she was shocked or saddened. She surrendered to a silence that razed the very foundations of the house. When Yusuf came home, she refused to see him or speak to him, and she avoided being in the same place with him. Then she started speaking of him in the third person as though he were deceased: 'Yusuf, may he rest in peace, used to say . . .' 'Remember, Malek, how Yusuf – may he rest in peace – used to come home late?' 'Yusuf – may he rest in peace – didn't like dark clothes.' 'Yusuf – may he rest in peace – used to like *Labaniya*.'

He thought about how, day after day, she had begun withering away from the inside. Yet he was helpless to extricate her and Yusuf – who had both capitulated to silence and melancholy – from the abyss into which they had fallen and flee with them to somewhere far away. For a moment it seemed to him that his mother had turned her back on life, unable to face it any longer because she'd lost certainty. She'd seen everything she thought she'd built over the years disintegrate suddenly before her very eyes. It tormented him to see her surrender to one ailment after another, but eventually he had no choice but to seek out the help of a woman who came three times a week to take care of the house, wash, cook and iron, breathing life into a household from which joy had absented itself because it was without a woman.

If his mother had been there, he would have buried his head in her lap and cried his heart out. But she wasn't there anymore. She'd withdrawn to the point of no return. She'd relieved herself of her burdens and begun visiting him in his dreams: smiling, calm and composed, yet without saying a word.

Sometimes he would ask her, 'How are you, Mom?'

Her only response was to smile that smile which, after some reflection, he realized was the smile of someone who's finally found rest because he *knows*. How he wished that he, too, *knew*, so that he could rest as well. But for years he hadn't even known what awaited him when he drove through an intersection at the end of some Medinan night; when, without meaning to, he stepped onto a sidewalk; or when he handed his residence card to someone who expected to see a national ID card. The most painful thing about these occasions was the tone of disapproval and disdain that he encountered: 'And a Camry 2001, too? What have you left for the country's own people?' 'You've cheated us with that robe of yours, and your *keffiyeh*!'

2:15 a.m.

Abu al-Hasan al-Asadi related to me on the authority of Muhammad ibn Salih ibn al-Nattah, on the authority of Abu al-Yaqazan, who heard Juwayriyah ibn Asma' say, "Abdullah ibn Ja'far received a slave by the name of al-Nusayb, whereupon he supplied him with a mount, gave him gifts, and clothed him. Then someone said to him, "Abu Ja'far, why have you given all these gifts to a black slave?" "By God," he replied, "although his skin is black, his heart is white, his poetry is in eloquent Arabic,

147

and for the lines he has composed he deserves more than what he has received. As for the gifts he has been given, they are nothing but she-camels that grow gaunt and feeble, garments that become old and tattered, and dirhems that are spent and consumed, whereas the praise he has earned will endure, and the eulogies he has composed will be recited for generations on end.'" (Abu al-Faraj al-Isfahani, *Kitab al-Aghani*)

I beg thee, long night, be gone and give way to morning, though the morning that follows thee will be nothing but more of the same! He let forth a faint, doleful laugh as he listened to his tone of voice in the stillness of the long night that had gone on without end, and weighed heavily upon him. The night that had given him its color but hadn't taken his sorrow from him. The night that, according to his mother, was the time when he'd been born, and in which he now hoped to die. The night in which he'd fallen so many years earlier, only to have an iron skewer pierce his chin, leaving a deep scar that ran diagonally from just beneath his lower lip, slightly right of center, to the tip of his chin. (On a number of occasions Leen had run her fingertips over it, telling him that she was 'charmed by it'.) The night at the end of which he didn't know what he would say to her or how he would say it. He couldn't tell her to stay, and he couldn't tell her to go. To tell her to stay would be selfish, and to tell her to go would be treacherous. Whichever he did, he would never stop blaming himself, and before he did either, he would have to listen to whatever she had to say.

What harm would there have been in their never meeting? What harm would there have been in his remaining the ten-year-old boy who used to leave the holy precincts after the Friday congregational prayer and go out by Bab al-Majidi, and who, drawn in by the first lines of *Awraq al-Ward* by Mustafa Sadiq al-Rafi'i, had stopped at the Dhiya' bookstore to buy the book? What harm would there have been in his continuing to sell refreshments and ice water to pilgrims and visitors to the city of pilgrims, at the shrines near the tomb of 'the chief of the martyrs', at the Seven Mosques, including the Mosque of the Two Qiblahs, and elsewhere?

Oh, God!

She'd known all the same neighborhoods, streets, alleys and seasons. But the two of them had met much later, which only made the anguish more devastating. There was no hope. Never since the time he met her had there been any hope. It was just that love had turned his being inside out, causing his fears, uncertainties and disappointments to settle to the bottom so that they stopped flashing like danger signals in the darkness of his long road. He realized now that hope – whose wiles he had tried to resist – had so subtly wrapped its snare about his feet that he hadn't noticed until the rope had tightened and drawn him in. So he found himself suspended in mid-air, swinging back and forth in a vast cold expanse with no reason to hope that anyone or anything might loosen the rope and give him a chance to escape.

But what was escape? At that moment it appeared that his only escape was to cry. But, ironically, he wasn't able to cry. He felt a lump in his throat that was about to choke him. This time it wasn't his lip but his heart that had been pierced with a red-hot skewer. And now it had begun gradually to cool down without his being able to pull it out or even budge it, since the shock of the pain was too great to be endured twice.

Yet, in spite of everything, he would never be able to distance himself from her or stop wanting her in the same way and to the same degree that he'd wanted her from the start. He would go on looking into her black eyes and wondering what his life had been like before encountering those eyes and where he'd been without them all that time. And why did he love her so? Did he love her because she was beautiful?

The neighbor girl Maryam had been beautiful, too, but he hadn't given her a chance. One evening she'd sent one of her little sisters to give him a carefully folded piece of paper. He still remembered the sky-blue color in which the message had been penned, the uneven letters, the hesitantly composed sentences, and the words '*I love you*' written with slanting letters. As he remembered her face, which he'd seen more than once, he'd felt a mysterious warmth flowing from the bottom of his stomach to the top of his throat. He realized that she had intended him to see her in the house when she visited his mother together with her mother, or through the door of their house when it was ajar. He had realized this, and his realization had been confirmed when he read her letter. But her beautiful face hadn't brought love. Love had remained behind a towering barrier that beauty alone hadn't been able to penetrate. He'd only said one thing to her. He'd spent long nights thinking about it in an attempt to ensure that it wouldn't be sharp or hurtful: 'I'm a man without a future, and you deserve better than that.'

But, if he didn't love Leen for her beauty, then did he love her because she was white?

He'd always rejected this suggestion, but when he did, he noticed that he would lose his composure like someone heatedly denying an accusation. He'd experienced being loved by a beautiful woman and gently turning her down because her beauty had done nothing to awaken what lay dormant inside him. But he'd never experienced being loved by a white woman – before Leen, that is – and gently turning her down because her whiteness hadn't touched him. It frightened him terribly because, when it came to her color, he had no history with which to compare his present experience. He wanted to believe that her color had nothing to do with his feelings. Consequently, he would sometimes have fantasies in which Leen was afflicted with some illness that changed her color, and at the critical moment when he discovered – in the fantasy – that her color had changed, he would ask himself theatrically, 'Will you still love her?' whereupon a long 'Yes' would resound inside him. However, he would pause in the face of that 'Yes' without being able to affirm it. He was sure he would still love her even if he were a different color. But what if *she* were a different color? Would he still love her? If so, then would he love her as much as he did now, or more, or less? If not, would it be because of her color and nothing else? And if he loved her, would his love for her be a victory for a torment that had nearly maimed his soul? Did he want to thumb his nose at the other color and say, 'She's left you and fallen in love with me!'? What if he asked her, 'Why do you love me?' How would she answer him? How would she look at the matter? What would she think he meant? Would she worry? And why, why did he torture himself with these questions and doubts?

He loved her. This was the certainty he possessed at that moment. He loved her because she was the way she was. He didn't know exactly what 'the way she was' meant. However, 'the way she was' was different. She resembled nothing and nobody but herself, and he was prepared – or, at least, he thought he was prepared – to take a risk in order for her to remain at his side, so that the feeling he experienced when he was with her – the feeling that he deserved to live – wouldn't leave him.

8

Google goes delirious

US and British forces launched several devastating raids yesterday evening and early this morning on Baghdad, which has been subjected to waves of airstrikes. According to an eye witness from Reuters, warning sirens could be heard all over Kuwait, auguring a possible rocket attack by Iraq. Meanwhile, the cities of Mosul, Kirkuk and Umm Qasr witnessed several explosions due to a spate of rockets fired by US forces. Newspaper reporters in Baghdad stated that explosions rocked Iraqi President Saddam Hussein's compound in the center of the capital, where pillars of smoke could be seen rising into the evening sky, and that fires had broken out throughout the area, which was hit by approximately ten rockets or bombs after 9 p.m. local time.

Shiyar ★ the 19th of al-Mu'tamar,
in the year of the Shock and Awe Campaign
3 a.m.

She pressed the 'Enter' key, the site opened, and the words were laid out before her in tidy, sharp relief against a pale green background. She quickly scanned the lines . . .

. . . There are words in classical Arabic which have become obsolete. Arabs have ceased using such words, as a result of which they have died out. They include, for example, the names of the days and months that were in use during the pre-Islamic era (the 'days of ignorance') . . .

Chapter One: Obsolete Names for the Days of the Week
The days of the week in the pre-Islamic era were as follows:

Sunday:	Awwal
Monday:	Ahwan and Awhad. Monday was also referred to as Yawm al-Thuna.
Tuesday:	Jubar
Wednesday:	Dubar or Dibar
Thursday:	Munis
Friday:	al-'Arubah and Harbah
Saturday:	Shiyar

These names then died out and were replaced with the names we know today: al-Sabt (Saturday), al-Ahad (Sunday), etc. A certain pre-Islamic poet gathered these names into verse, saying:

> I hope to live, but my dying day
> will be Awwal, Ahwan or Jubar.
> Otherwise it will be the next day, Dubar,
> and if I survive that day as well,
> then Munis, 'Arubah or Shiyar.
> These are the days of our earthly plight,
> With night overtaking day, and day, night.

Chapter Two: Obsolete Names for the Months of the Year
The names of the lunar months in the pre-Islamic era were as follows:

Al-Muharram:	al-Mu'tamar
Safar:	Najir
Rabi' al-Awwal:	Khawwan or Khuwwan
Rabi al-Akhir:	Wubsan or Wabsan
Jumada al-Ula:	al-Hanin
Jumada al-Akhirah:	Runna or Rubba
Rajab:	al-Asamm
Sha'ban:	'Adhil
Ramadan:	Natiq
Shawwal:	Wail
Dhu al-Qa'dah:	Warnah or Huwa'
Dhu al-Hijjah:	Burak

There are scholars who disagree with the majority view on the names of these months. Biruni, for example, listed them as follows: al-Mu'tamar, Najir, Khawwan, Suwan, Hantim, Zabba', al-Asamm, 'Adil, Nafiq, Waghil, Huwa', and Burak. As for Sahib ibn 'Abbad, he organized them poetically as follows:

If you wish to know how Arabs named
their months in the days of ignorance,
I shall list them for you from the beginning.
Just as we now begin with al-Muharram:
First comes Mu'tamar, then Najir,
Then Khawwan and Suwan in an inseparable duo.
Then Hanin with Zaba, al-Asamm,'Adil,
Nafiq with Waghl and Warnah with Burak.

A comparison between these names and their counterparts in the lists given by Biruni and Sahib ibn 'Abbad gives us good reason to believe that some of them have been misspelled or corrupted. Compare, for example, Wabsan and Suwwan; al-Hanin and Hantim; Rubba, Runna and Zabba'; 'Adhil and 'Adil; Natiq and Nafiq; Wail and Waghil. It comes as no surprise that the names of these months should have undergone corruption given the fact that they dropped out of usage so long ago and were rendered obsolete. The differences may also reflect tribal dialects.

Al-Mas'udi presented a listing that differed in some respects. He listed the pre-Islamic names of the months as: Natiq, Thaqil, Taliq, Najir, Aslakh, Amyah, Ahlak, Kusa', Zahir, Burak, Huraf and Nuas; that is, Dhu al-Hijjah.

. . .

The Arabs derived the well-known names of al-Muharram, Safar, etc., from events that happened to occur at the time the namings took place. It will thus be apparent to whoever reflects on the derivation of the names of the months in the pre-Islamic era (the 'days of ignorance') and the names that came into use later that a long time passed between the two namings of each month given the differing significations each name bears with respect to the specific events associated with the month concerned.

She sat back in her chair, pondering the near-darkness in her room. The only source of lighting was her computer screen. Sighing dejectedly, she closed her eyes and thought about Malek's face as he lay in his state of oblivion. She also thought about the war that was going to devour so many things. She'd lived through two wars without Malek. She didn't know whether this was a good sign or a bad one. However, she believed it was a sign. Then it dawned on her – with painful slowness – that everything had been clear from the beginning. It had come and gone before her eyes, but she hadn't wanted to see. She'd been looking at things without seeing. Or she had seen, but had chosen to disregard what she saw. Now everything was laughing at her in derision, and she couldn't say, 'That's enough!'

She copied what was on the screen, then went to 'Word' and pasted it there. After formatting it to print it out, she pressed the 'Printer' icon on the toolbar. The printer revved up loudly and started to shudder as though it were having convulsions. She took the sheet of paper that had come out of the printer and stuck it with a colored thumbtack onto a Styrofoam bulletin board over her desk. Then she stood there contemplating it.

For a few moments she saw the days and months removing their masks before her very eyes and revealing their old faces.

She saw Shiyar shedding its Sabt, Awwal shedding its Ahad, 'Adhil shedding its Sha'ban, and Wa'il shedding its Shawwal. The old faces weren't ugly. They were just wrinkled from having perspired for so long beneath masks that didn't belong to them. When she saw this happening, she thought everything had finally been straightened out. It was all she could think about anymore. She could no longer close her ears to the loud clamor that filled her head, leading her to the wreckage she'd been fleeing from for so long:

I remembered someone weeping over me, but found no on . . . / Disappointed. / Heh heh heh he-e-e-e-e-e-e-e-h heh heh heh! / The rain doesn't come during the day anymore. / Girls are fire. Thank God I don't have any! / The Carter Doctrine. / I love you, you've hated me. / Cursed. / He danced with me. / If I die and am raised again. / So you think you're going to fix the world, smarty pants? Just have a good time! / For heaven's sake, aren't you ashamed of yourself? / Heh heh heh he-e-e-e-e-e-e-e-h heh heh heh! / And if you leave me, I won't die. / Stupid. / I can't, Leen! / *. . . who causes His angels to be His message-bearers, endowed with wings, two or three or four . . .* / Crazy. / Fear thrives on ignorance. / *Let no one treat us unjustly, lest we prove ourselves to be more unjust than the unjust themselves.* / There's no cure for love. / Heh heh heh he-e-e-e-e-e-e-h heh heh heh! / She must have done something wrong with him. Otherwise, why would she insist on marrying him? / Mercy has abandoned me. / We're on the brink of war. / *Wrong done by near-of-kin is more heartbreaking.* / Your eyes are twinkling. / Watch out for Arab girls, son. You'll see they can't be trusted. / *I remembered you as the spears were* *drinking their fill.* / The Saudis just play around with money. / Heh heh heh he-e-e-e-e-e-e-e-h heh heh heh! / Hey, girl, you're not a Bedouin, so why do you go around with Hejazi girls? / I was dead. / The mask fell off. / *God is greater, and away with the despicable outcasts!* / If I could stop being in love. / The sound of metal grating against metal disturbs me. / Come, let's plant a tree. / Oh Lord, why did you create color? / Be mine. / Two swords uprooting a palm tree. / The sugar says to the tea, 'Ugh, you're black!' / Heh heh heh he-e-e-e-e-e-e-e-h heh heh heh! / *They say, 'Perish not for sorrow, rather, adorn thyself with patient endurance.'* / Have you seen the make-up they've started wearing to wakes? It's really something! / I might die tomorrow. / The Americans think the Iraqis are going to welcome their troops with flowers. / *I beg thee, long night, be gone and give way to morning . . .* / Yearning glows like a star that will soon go out. / I lose without hope. / Your eyes are black like my night. / Oh Lord, protect me against the wiles of hope. / *That's right, we are the Hejaz, and we are Nejd.* / *Draw the sword without fear or dread.* / *Draw the sword without fear or dread.* / *Draw the sword without fear or dread.* / *Draw the sword without fear or dread.* / *Draw the sword without fear or dread.* / *Draw the sword without fear or dread . . .*

Glossary

'Absolution': The term with which Malek refers sardonically to the coveted Saudi citizenship, thereby implying that to lack such citizenship is to be tainted with some sort of 'sin'.

Adhan: The call to Islamic prayer issued by a muezzin five times a day.

Bab al-Majidi: Prior to being razed under orders from King Fahd in 1984 to allow for the expansion of the Prophet's Mosque in Medina, the neighborhood known as Bab al-Majidi was located adjacent to the mosque gate known by the same name – Bab al-Majidi. Bab al-Majidi (the Majidi Gate) was named after the Ottoman Sultan 'Abd al-Majid, who renovated the Prophet's Mosque in the year 1277 AH/1860 CE.

Baqaya Hujjaj: Meaning something on the order of 'the remnants of pilgrims', the term *Baqaya Hujjaj* is used to refer contemptuously to people of non-Saudi origin, whose ancestors came to the Arabian Peninsula to perform the *hajj*, or pilgrimage to Mecca, and who never returned to their home countries. (See *Tarsh Bahr* below.)

Biruni: Abu Rayhan al-Biruni (d. 440 AH/1048 CE in Ghazni, Afghanistan) was a Persian polymath now considered to be one of the greatest Muslim scholars of the medieval period. He distinguished himself in particular as a historian, chronologist and linguist.

Carter Doctrine: The 'Carter Doctrine' (so named for its association with President Jimmy Carter), set forth by the US government in January 1980, served as the basis for the formation of military forces for rapid deployment and intervention in the Arab Gulf region. In articulating the Carter Doctrine, the US government expressed its concern over the dangers that threatened it and its allies in the Arab Gulf and asserted its determination to resist by all possible means, including the use of armed force, any attempt by any foreign state to control the region.

Chief of the martyrs: An epithet given to the Prophet Muhammad's paternal uncle, Hamzah ibn 'Abd al-Muttalib, who died as a martyr at the Battle of Uhud in the year 3 AH/625 CE.

Dome of the Prophet: The green dome over the center of al-Masjid al-Nabawi, or the Prophet's Mosque in Medina, where the Prophet's tomb is located.

Draw the sword . . .: These words form part of the opening verse of a poem composed by the late Iraqi President Saddam Hussein, who recited it over the air to the Iraqi people on the day when the 2003 US invasion of Iraq began.

Falata and Hausa tribes: The Falata tribe is found in Sudan and other West African countries, while the Hausa tribe is one of the five major tribes of Nigeria.

Family book: A booklet that contains a married man's name, national identification number and place of residence, the name of his mother, and the names and national identification numbers of his wife (or wives) and children.

Fatihah: The first chapter (*surah*) of the Qur'an. Recited at the beginning of every ritual prayer in Islam, the *Fatihah* reads: 'In the name of God, Most Gracious, Most Merciful. Praise be to God, the Cherisher and Sustainer of the worlds; Most Gracious, Most Merciful; Master of the Day of Judgment. Thee do we worship, and thine aid do we seek. Show us the straight way, the way of those on whom Thou hast bestowed Thy grace, those whose portion is not wrath, and who go not astray.'

Gagarin's orbit around the Earth: A Soviet cosmonaut, Yuri Gagarin (1934–68), was the first human to travel into outer space, and on April 12, 1961 he orbited the Earth in a Vostok spacecraft.

God is greater, and away with . . .: A phrase used frequently by Saddam Hussein in his speeches during the US invasion of Iraq.

Hajji: An honorific title given to someone who has completed the *hajj*, or major pilgrimage to Mecca. It is also used as a term of respectful address for an older man one doesn't know.

Hamam al-barr: A dish made of chickpea flour, salt and various seasonings.

Hasbi Allah wa ni'm al-wakil: A phrase meaning 'God is sufficient for me, and the perfect Guardian'. These words are often uttered when someone is in a distressing situation.

I beg thee, long night . . .: Taken from the *Mu'allaqah* of pre-Islamic poet Imru' al-Qays.

Ibn Hesham: Ibn Hesham (d. 218 AH/833 CE) is best known for his recension of Ibn Ishaq's *al-Sirah al-Nabawiyah* (a biography of the Prophet Muhammad), which is no longer extant.

Iqama: The muezzin's announcement that one of the five Islamic ritual prayers is commencing in the mosque.

I remembered someone weeping over me . . .: From an elegy composed for himself by the poet Malek ibn al-Rayb al-Tamimi (d. 57 AH/676 CE).

I remembered you as the spears . . .: From an ode by pre-Islamic poet and adventurer 'Antarah ibn Shaddad al-'Absi (d. 608 CE).

January 17, 1991: The first day of Operation Desert Storm, a war waged against Iraq in response to the latter's invasion and annexation of Kuwait. The operation was carried out by a UN-authorized, US-led coalition force from thirty-four countries.

Kur: A racial slur used against black Arabs, similar to terms such as 'coon', 'jiggaboo', 'nigger' and the like.

Kuwayha: See entry for *kur* above.

Labaniya: A kind of dessert made from dried milk, sugar, water, butter and cardamom, cut into squares and sprinkled with pistachios.

La hawla wa la quwwata illa billah: Meaning 'There is no power or strength save in God', the phrase *la hawla wa la quwwata illa billah* is uttered when someone is facing a difficult or painful situation.

Let no one treat us unjustly . . . : A line taken from the *Mu'allaqah* of pre-Islamic poet 'Amr ibn Kulthum (d. 584 CE).

Majed Abdullah: Born in 1959, Majed Abdullah is a former Saudi Arabian soccer player. An all-time top striker for the Saudi national team, he has been referred to as the Arabian Pelé.

Manfoush: A kind of fry bread of South Asian origin.

Mushabbak: A Middle Eastern pastry made from a wheat-flour dough shaped into rings which are then fried and dipped in syrup.

Mustafa Sadiq al-Rafi'i: An Egyptian poet of Syrian origin, Mustafa Sadiq al-Rafi'i was born in Egypt in January 1880 and died in May 1937. He wrote the lyrics of the Egyptian national anthem which was used from 1923 to 1936, as well as the lyrics of Tunisia's current national anthem.

'One, One, One . . .' (Arabic, ahad, ahad, ahad): Bilal is insistently affirming God's perfect oneness and uniqueness. The term *ahad* is found in Surah 112, which reads, 'Say: He is God, the One and

Only (*ahad*), God, the Eternal, Absolute; He begetteth not, nor is He begotten, and there is none like unto Him.' (Abdullah Yusuf Ali's translation)

Picnic: The Arabic word translated as 'picnic' here is derived from the name of the month of Sha'ban, which immediately precedes the fasting month of Ramadan. The type of picnic referred to is thus a kind of pre-Ramadan celebration as well, and a long-standing Hejazi custom.

Rafig (rafiq): The term *rafiq* means 'friend' or 'companion'. However, it is used by Saudis to refer to Indians in a depreciatory sense. The Saudis may in fact have taken this term from the Indians themselves, who, following the Muslim conquests of the Indian subcontinent between the thirteenth and sixteenth centuries CE, introduced numerous Arabic terms into their speech, including the use of *rafiq* to refer to their friends and associates.

Sahib ibn 'Abbad: Sahib ibn 'Abbad (d. 385 AH/995 CE) was the vizier and *littérateur* of Mu'ayyad al-Dawlah, the Buwayhid emir of Hamadan (d. 373 AH/983 CE).

Serbs: In response to tribal Saudis who refer derisively to some residents of the Hejaz (in Western Saudi Arabia) as *Tarsh Bahr* ('refuse from the sea') and *Baqaya Hujjaj* ('leftover pilgrims'), some Hejazis refer to tribal Saudis as *Badu Sirb* ('Serbian Bedouins'). *Badu Sirb* is a relatively recent term, referring back to the war that broke out in Bosnia-Herzegovina in 1992 and lasted until December, 1995. In the course of this conflict, the Serbs committed horrific atrocities against the area's Muslim Bosniak population. *Badu Sirb* is thus a racial slur which implies that the tribal Saudis (Bedouins) would have no compunctions about committing the most heinous brutalities.

Seven Mosques: A reference to Medina's most famous seven mosques. Five of these mosques are associated, respectively, with Fatimah, the Prophet Muhammad's daughter; 'Ali ibn Abi Talib, the Prophet's cousin, son-in-law and fourth caliph; Abu Bakr, a companion of the Prophet and the first caliph; 'Umar ibn al-Khattab, companion of the Prophet and the second caliph; and Salman al-Farisi, a companion of the Prophet. The other two are the Fath Mosque (built on the spot where the Prophet Muhammad said that the Qur'an had first been revealed to him), and the Mosque of the Two Qiblahs.

Surat al-Hashr: Chapter 59 of the Qur'an.

Takruni: A racial slur used to refer to black Arabs. See entries for *kur* and *kuwayha* above.

Tarsh Bahr: Meaning something like 'what the sea spit up', the term *Tarsh Bahr* is a racist epithet used by some Saudis who belong to tribes indigenous to the Arabian Peninsula as a way of expressing contempt for Hejazis who do not belong to Arabian tribes. Many of these Hejazis are descended from people who came to Mecca to perform the hajj, or major pilgrimage, after which they either remained in Mecca or traveled to Medina in order to visit the Prophet's Mosque, then chose to stay there in order to live in close proximity to the Prophet Muhammad. These individuals trace their roots to countries in Central and East Asia, India, Afghanistan, and numerous African states such as Niger, Nigeria, Mali and Somalia.

That's right, we are the Hejaz, and we are Nejd: A phrase from a poem written by the late Saudi Arabian politician, intellectual and *littérateur* Ghazi Al Gosaibi (1940-2010) during the war to liberate Kuwait following its invasion by Iraq. The poem was a response to attempts on the part of the Iraqi regime to bring about divisions among the Saudis and propose a partitioning of Saudi territory.

They say, 'Perish not . . .': From the *Mu'allaqah* of Imru' al-Qays.

Yahya: The Yahya referred to in the account taken from *al-Kamil fil al-Tarikh* (5:424) by Ibn al-Athir is Yahya ibn Muhammad, brother of the notorious Abbasid caliph Abu al-'Abbas (whose caliphate lasted from 132–137 AH/749–754 CE). When the people of Mosul refused to obey Muhammad ibn Sul, who had been appointed governor over them by the Abbasids, Caliph Abu al-'Abbas sent his brother, Yahya ibn Muhammad, against the people of Mosul at the head of 12,000 men, and they carried out a heinous slaughter in the city.

'. . . who causes His angels . . .': Taken from Surah 35:1.

Wrong done by near-of-kin . . .: A phrase taken from the *Mu'allaqah* of sixth-century pre-Islamic poet Tarafah ibn al-'Abd.

A Note on the Author

Laila Aljohani is an award-winning Saudi Arabian writer of short stories and novels. She was born in the northern city of Tabuk, Saudi Arabia. She is the author of *Always Love Will Remain* (1995), which won second place at the Abha Prize for Culture, *The Barren Paradise* (1998), which won first place at Sharjah Prize for Arab Creativity, and was translated to Italian, *Days of Ignorance* (2007) and *40 Fi Ma'ana An Akbur* (2009).

Days of Ignorance is the first of her novels to be translated into English.

A Note on the Translator

Nancy Roberts' literary translations include *Beirut '75* by Ghada Samman, for which she won the Arkansas Arabic Translation Award, and *The Man from Bashmour* by Salwa Bakr, for which she received a commendation from the judges of the 2008 Saif Ghobash–Banipal Prize.

A Note on the Type

The text of this book is set in Bembo. This type was first used in 1495 by the Venetian printer Aldus Manutius for Cardinal Bembo's *De Aetna*, and was cut for Manutius by Francesco Griffo. It was one of the types used by Claude Garamond (1480–1561) as a model for his Romain de L'Université, and so it was the forerunner of what became standard European type for the following two centuries. Its modern form follows the original types and was designed for Monotype in 1929.